NIKHIL AND RIYA

Ira Trivedi is the author of six books, including *India in Love*. When she is not writing, she is doing yoga. She lives in New Delhi. For more information visit her website www.iratrivedi.in

Nikhil and Riya

IRA TRIVEDI

HARLEQUIN INDIA PVT LTD

First published in India in 2016 by Harlequin
An imprint of HarperCollins *Publishers*

P-ISBN: 978-93-5264-130-7
E-ISBN: 978-93-5264-131-4

2 4 6 8 10 9 7 5 3 1

HarperCollins *Publishers*
A-75, Sector 57, Noida, Uttar Pradesh 201301, India
1 London Bridge Street, London, SE1 9GF, United Kingdom
Hazelton Lanes, 55 Avenue Road, Suite 2900, Toronto, Ontario M5R 3L2
and 1995 Markham Road, Scarborough, Ontario M1B 5M8, Canada
25 Ryde Road, Pymble, Sydney, NSW 2073, Australia
195 Broadway, New York, NY 10007, USA

Typeset in 11/14.2 Adobe Caslon Pro
by Saanvi Graphics Noida

Printed and bound at
Thomson Press (India) Ltd

To Nikhil and Riya. Thank you for coming alive.

'Never say goodbye, because saying goodbye means going away and going away means forgetting' – J.M. Barrie, *Peter Pan*

'Goodbyes are only for those who love with their eyes. Because for those who love with their heart and soul there is no such thing as separation' – Rumi

'Sometimes you hear a voice through the door calling you … This turning towards what you deeply love saves you' – Rumi

ALWAYS

You were you,
And I was I
We were two
Before our time

I was yours
Before I knew
And you have always
Been mine too

– Anonymous

Part 1

1

'SPECS, YOUR SUM is wrong.'

'My name is Nikhil,' I replied. 'The sum is right, your answer is not. And I can't understand your handwriting.'

'You're crazy, Specs! My handwriting is fine. You just need to get your eyes checked.'

I crossed my arms over my chest and looked at her. 'You know that I'm doing you a favour by teaching you, right?'

'You're a teacher's pet, aren't you, Specs?' she teases, balancing on one leg, pulling up her white sock.

Sometimes I had to remind her who was in charge. 'No, Riya, I'm just trying to help you out. Rao Ma'am sometimes asks me to help weak students out.'

'I'm not a weak student,' she says proudly, standing still now, hands on her tiny waist.

'You got a two in your last maths exam. Out of hundred.'

That seems to shut her up. She sits down on the bench, picks up her pen and locks her eyes with mine. They are humorous and compassionate and so alive that I can't help but stare…

Suddenly my eyes open wide and my gaze goes straight to the clock on my bedside.

10.00 a.m.

10.00 a.m.!

I throw off the sheets and scramble to my feet.

'Damn it, Meeta! Why didn't you wake me up?' Even though I am half-asleep, I know I am unnecessarily harsh.

My heavily pregnant wife waddles in and stands by the bedroom door, alarmed. 'You were sleeping so soundly. Plus, you came home so late last night.'

I ignore her and rush to the bathroom, slamming the door shut.

Minutes later, my hair still dripping wet, I sit down at the breakfast table and stare at my toast. There is no point in hurrying now; I have missed the meeting by a long shot. I read the papers and glance around the apartment, a pinnacle of corporate success – German fittings, Japanese toilets, the best pincode in town. These trappings usually make me happy, but today they don't help.

I notice the remains of my son's breakfast. He has already left for school and I realize with a pang that it's been three days since I saw my little boy. I remind myself that this was to be expected, especially after my promotion to partner, the youngest in the history of the bank.

I think of the meeting again and immediately feel a sense of dread.

'Can you still make it to the meeting?' asks Meeta, bringing me a cup of tea.

'It's too late now.'

'Was it important?' she asks, concerned.

'Very,' I say, trying to keep the disappointment out of my voice. But she, my wife, never misses a beat.

'It can't be *that* important to put you in such a bad mood,' she teases.

'You couldn't possibly understand how much that meeting was worth.'

The words are sharper than I mean. Meeta, pouring my tea, says nothing. Why do I always do this? Why do I try to make her feel like she is a silly housewife when we both know that she is not? An apology crawls to the tip of my tongue, but I quickly swallow it back.

Instead, I make an effort to mend my mistake: 'When is the doctor's next appointment?'

'Tomorrow.'

'Time?' I realize that I have missed seven out of the last ten appointments. Guilt scalds me. For the hundredth time, the thousandth time, I know that I am a bad husband.

'I'll check,' she says, scrambling to her feet, relieved to see my mood lift.

'No worries. Just text me or send me a Google invite.'

'Google invite?' she says, confused.

'Never mind. Just tell someone at the office, they'll punch it in.'

I get up, brushing the crumbs off my freshly pressed shirt. Meeta, ever dutiful, picks up my dirty plate.

As I am about to leave, something in the newspaper catches my eye. For a second, I can't believe it. I stare and then blink very hard, reaching for the newspaper, dropping the glass I am drinking from. I sputter and choke on the water that I have quickly gulped down, my eyes fixed on an obituary with an unmistakable picture underneath.

2

THE FAMILIARITY OF his face takes my breath away and suddenly all those years seem to melt away. I had pushed these memories into the deepest recesses of my mind, but now they are back and it feels like nails being drilled into a wall. I feel a pain in my left leg so sharp that I have to sit down, and suddenly it is as if I am fifteen again. I am back there and the smoke is rising like a plume into the sky. I keep reaching out to catch it, but it is too far away and disappears into the clouds. Memories flash: the wind, a bird, cracked glasses, frozen leg.

My wife rushes in, concern flooding her face as she looks at the shards of glass covering the floor.

'What is it?' she asks in a whisper.

'Nothing,' I mumble, tearing my mind away from the past.

'I see,' she says, unconvinced. She looks at me, waiting for an answer. I know I cannot avoid this.

'Someone I knew. He died,' I finally say, clearing my throat, trying to regain composure, pointing to the paper in front of me.

'Who?' she cautiously asks.

'An old teacher of mine.'

She comes and puts her arm on my shoulder. I stiffen at her touch. It is the last thing that could have helped.

'From Stephen's?'

'No. From school.'

'You never talk about school,' she says, looking at me with her large, kind eyes.

I want to close the newspaper and simply walk away, but I am frozen and in excruciating pain. I know without a doubt that I cannot ignore this, like I have done everything about Residency School for seventeen long years. It is B.P.'s funeral and I simply have to go.

'Meeta,' I slowly say, thoughts in my brain exploding like cannonballs. 'Can you please pack me a bag?'

3

THEY STAND THERE waiting to bid me farewell, his little hand in her large one, him a replica of her, them a complete family of two. It occurs to me that they do not need me, nor that they really know me. He is sleepy – this is his naptime – and she is very concerned. She is used to my calculated, balanced ways. And now, I am suddenly running off for the funeral of an old school teacher, when she has never heard me even speak about school.

I kiss her gruffly. 'Let me know what the doc says?' I smile an exaggerated smile – like a cheery buffoon – for my son. And then I depart.

On the outside, I am the picture of authority and calm, a look and demeanour I have perfected through years of corporate life. On the inside, I am feeling so much that I am almost numb. I haven't been back to Residency School since the day I left seventeen years ago. Now it is all coming back to me in a nauseating wave – B.P.'s calm and patient smile, the sounds of small feet and big bells, the smell of notebooks and ink, the red sand from the track hitting my face like sea spray, the mountains that rose like sharp teeth, the constellations like needles in the sky, and always, in every moment, in every memory, there is her.

Before I reach the highway, I stop at a small temple by the roadside. I get out of my car and stand in front of the idols and stare at the flames. Engulfed by the smell of flowers, milk and grime, I close my eyes. People stream in and out, but I am lost in a prayer, until the pundit touches my forehead and I open my eyes in surprise. He looks at me, greedy and imploring, and I give him the notes I clutch in my hand.

I get back into the car and drive, the road now clear, the traffic far behind. The landscape changes fast: from the dense urban settlements, I am now coming upon large tracts of lifeless sulphur yellow land lined with fading trees. And suddenly it is 1989 and I am a five-year-old orphan with a crippled leg, and it is time now to take the journey I never thought I would have the courage for.

4

I REALIZE THAT my head is pounding and my stomach is churning. I haven't eaten all day. I drive for a while longer and then stop at the same rest stop that I have stopped at on every journey up the hills for fifteen years. I'm mildly surprised by how much it has changed. Back then it was an outdoor dhaba serving steaming chai in flimsy plastic cups that melted in our hands as we drank sitting on string cots. Now it is all cement and plastic and neon and glass.

This is a popular road, and the rest stop is crowded with boarding school students, shivering with the excitement of a new session about to begin. I am surprised at the number of girls I see. Back then, most boarding schools were all boys. But now, girls are everywhere, giggling in the way only schoolgirls do, and I think to myself that although their thick, broadcloth skirts have got distinctly shorter, everything else about them remains very much the same: the chatter, the long hair braided with ribbons, the coltish legs, the shy glances they throw at the boys.

Amidst the eager young crowds, I manage to get a seat in a corner where I can sit for a few minutes with my lunch. Once, this greasy burger oozing fluorescent ketchup would have been a treat, but today I eat it out of compulsion, and I am annoyed at Meeta for not packing my protein shake and sandwiches. I remind myself that she is heavily pregnant, with a three-year-old to raise. I scold myself for being so unfair. Sometimes I don't understand why I always blame her for everything.

I sit uncomfortably close to a young couple so in love that they hardly notice me. They hold hands underneath the table, feeding each other bits of a muffin, smiling bashfully.

'When did you first fall in love with me?' the girl asks the boy.

'The moment I saw you, of course.'

'Oh, shut up! You did not. You didn't even notice me.'

'Of course I did,' he protests.

'What was I wearing?' she contests with puckered lips.

'That nice pink salwar kameez of yours.'

'Liar. Just because I like pink! It was my blue chikan kurta, and I had flowers in my hair!'

'No,' he says. 'That was the second time I saw you. The first time I saw you was in your Facebook pic, and you were wearing pink.'

Kids these days, I think, rolling my eyes as I stand up to leave.

5

I COULD NEVER forget the first time I saw her, no matter how hard I ever tried.

Tenth standard, Prem Ma'am's second period history class.

The class, as usual, was chaotic. Under Prem Ma'am's weak authority, even the most disciplined girls misbehaved. At the back of the class, the boys, led by Vikram, tried to squash a little green lizard that had snuck up the wall.

This was a strain as I sat at the back of the musty, echoing classroom, struggling to hear Prem Ma'am's lousy dictations, desperately making notes in not just my notebook, but in Vikram's too, the splintered wooden desk, at least a hundred years old, wobbling as I scribbled in haste. The class was getting wilder by the minute as Prem Ma'am stood sputtering in the front of the room, her white bra visible through her thin muslin blouse.

And then, suddenly, the class went silent, probably more silent than it had ever been in the history of Prem Ma'am's history period. I was relieved to take this time to complete the dictation, the wobbles of my desk the loudest sound in the room.

'Prem Ma'am?' said a voice at the door.

'Yes?' said Prem Ma'am, turning around, pallu falling off her neck, her hands full of chalk dust. Ordinarily this would have induced laughter. Not today. The newcomer walked in and handed Prem Ma'am a note which she hastily read, her glasses slipping down her nose.

'Riya. Riya Pratap. Welcome to Residency School.'

Then she turned towards the class.

'Children, it's her first day on campus, please say hello.'

'Heeellooo, Riyaaa,' chimed the class, the boys grinning, the girls giggling. None of them had welcomed a student like this since the second standard.

This was when I, finally, looked up. And this was also when my whole life changed.

She stood in front of the chalk-streaked blackboard, her hair tied at the nape of her neck, spilling down her back in a messy ponytail. Her blue skirt was too short. Her white shirt was transparent, and she wasn't wearing a slip underneath. Her white socks fell far below the knee, where they were required to be.

The girl standing at the front of the class was different from anyone or anything that I had ever seen in my life. The sight of her was so striking that I dropped my pen. And stared and stared and stared.

Then I felt a slap on my back, and snapped out of my reverie.

'Oi, what are *you* looking at?' Vikram whispered in my ear, a crooked smile on his lips.

I mumbled something and pretended to go back to my notebook. Then I used every ounce of my self-control to try not to look at her. But I failed; I simply could not tear my eyes away. She stood haughty and nervous in front of the class, straight as an arrow, her chin up in the air, her eyes the darkest shade of brown, her lips the deepest shade of red. She had long brown legs and thighs so strong that they were visible even under her thick pleated skirt. I remember thinking, *She can probably run well.* I was wrong. She ran like the wind.

6

IT SEEMS APPROPRIATE to start her story, our story, with my own. My parents died in a car crash when I was four years old. My memories of them consist entirely of the three fuzzy pictures enclosed in a glass cupboard in my grandparents' house. Them, at their wedding; them, on holiday; them, with baby Nikhil, everyone beaming. Otherwise, I simply do not remember the two people who gave me life – the father whose heart-shaped face I had inherited and the mother whose doe eyes everyone said I had.

After the accident I lived with my father's parents, my only surviving grandparents, who were so ancient and dotty that they couldn't cope with both their grief and their five-year-old grandson simultaneously. And so it was me they chose to get rid of, packing me off to boarding school a year after I had arrived.

The lingering memory that I have of my first few years at Residency School is of gentle, melancholic sadness. I was a quiet boy of five, prone to high fevers, crying and hiding in dark corners. The kind junior school matron dried my tears, held me close and dragged me out from under the bed. She gave me hard-boiled candies so sweet they made my head spin and whispered that I would be fine, that here I would have many mothers, many fathers, and many brothers who would be with me till the end of my life.

I believed her, I really did. I was only a sickly child who sucked his thumb and occasionally wet his bed. But I never did find any of the things that she had promised – not once in the thirteen years I spent at this school. The teachers never became my mothers or my fathers, and the boys never became my brothers. But later on, none of it mattered, because I had her and she became everything that I ever needed and that I had never known.

I too had been in the accident with my parents. They had died and I had been left with a battered left leg and a heavy limp. My grandparents, in their grief, had missed the crucial fact that they were sending their crippled grandson to a school where life revolved around sports that I would never be able to play. But I never blamed them; in fact, I would only later find out that it had taken the entirety of my dead father's pension to send me to Residency School.

7

RESIDENCY SCHOOL WAS a product of its time, established in 1867 by the resident governor of the erstwhile British Raj to educate the children of the Indian princely states. After Independence, keeping with the ethos of a free India, the board of governors of Residency School opened the school to one and all, envisioning an educational institution that would be entirely secular for boys from all sections of society and from every state, who would then go on to serve a free and democratic India. Residency School was a rock, a bulwark, a steady hand. Our motto was 'Unchanging, Unending, Unflinching'.

I know and I can recite this information verbatim because every Residency student was made to memorize this. I am not sure how many of our boys went on to 'serve India' but many of them became star sportsmen and athletes.

As we got older, everything about being a boy at Residency School became about sports. Growing up meant progressing from the under-14s, to the under-16s, to the under-18s. I loved books, drawing and multiplication. They loved cricket, football and drills. Sportsmen were heroes and I couldn't even run.

But I did train myself. I trained myself to feel little or nothing at all when I couldn't play with others, when they laughed at me or teased me about my limp, I turned inward, tuning out their jibes. If they were cruel, I would simply walk away; if they were playing a game, I made the best of it by watching quietly from the sidelines. When I got lonely, I found refuge in a book.

I had my own havens. I loved the library, and I loved mathematics. I discovered early on that I had a knack for numbers. I could visualize numbers in my head, solve in seconds sums that nobody else could. So while the other boys played football, cricket and squash, I played with formulae and from my early days, I was the best student in Residency School.

And so over the years, I found my role within the complex school ecosystem. I was the boy people could come to for completing their homework, the boy who could always be counted on to pass chits during the exams. I wasn't at the bottom of the pyramid, but somewhere in the shadows, so much a part of the landscape that I almost merged in with the red brick walls.

8

OBJECTIVELY, RIYA WASN'T beautiful – at least not the way actresses were, or the sort of way the women in the magazines stashed under hostel beds were. Even though I was hardly an expert on the fairer sex, none of the tenth-standard girls struck me as being particularly pretty – they weren't girls, nor women, but stuck somewhere in an uncomfortable place in between. They all looked the same to me. Most had angry pimples and walked awkwardly, hunched, to hide their budding chests.

Not Riya. She was tall and straight, her heart-shaped face bright and clear, a small nose perched above her perfect rose-shaped lips. And those eyes, those maddening eyes. Not quite black, but the deepest shade of brown, like the wet leaves that piled up under the deodar trees in the monsoon. And her hair. Most of the girls wore tight braids, but Riya almost always had a loose ponytail, which looked copper in the sun.

The first time I saw her, I was drawn like a magnet, hopelessly and shamelessly ensnared. From then on no matter how hard I tried I couldn't help but stare at her – as she walked in and out of the classroom, her blue skirt swishing around her long brown legs; as she gazed, utterly bored, out of the window during class, her dimpled chin in her palms. She had a haughty, glorious smile. She spoke slowly, in a sing-song sort of a way. Her eyebrows moved around her face like the wings of a beautiful bird.

Day and night she danced about my brain – from the moment I woke up, as I sat through class, when I did my homework, as I walked around campus during games period. Thinking about her wasn't enough, so eventually I began dreaming about her, and I had dreams so vivid that sometimes I thought that she was actually there. I would cling to these dreams even when I woke up, confused and upset to be back in my clapboard bed in the dormitory, surrounded by the sighs and snuffles of so many boys.

I had never ever felt like this before. I had begun finding girls attractive a few years ago, but not like this. This feeling, it was something else. Something that I did not understand, something that I could not rationalize, something that drove me totally out of my mind. I started doing things that shocked even me, but I couldn't help it – it was as if there was another force that controlled me. I pocketed pens she had left behind, picked up the scraps of paper she had written on and thrown away. I spied on her on every occasion that I could, lurking around the classroom when she was there, doing unnecessary things just so I could be around her. Once I even contemplated, but did not execute, retrieving the chewing gum from the dustbin that she had been ordered to spit out. That piece of gum had touched her lips, had swirled in her mouth, had sat on her tongue.

Although Riya and I were in the same class, she barely registered my presence and I never, not once, had the nerve to talk to her. I usually sat in the middle of the classroom – the closest that boys could safely be to the front of the classroom, without getting teased. She was all the way at the front, under the nose of the teachers because she was always getting into trouble for falling asleep, for daydreaming, for being late, for being the poor student that she was.

Somehow I didn't mind watching her from afar. I'd always been on the sidelines at this school and I happily fell into the same habit with her, the thought of actually stepping onto the playing field completely foreign to me.

9

RIYA'S FATHER WAS Bhanu Pratap, popularly known as B.P., the sports director and cricket coach on campus. This was an important position in a school that had been the IPSC (Indian Public School Competition) champion for ten straight years. B.P. was a well-known cricket player, a Ranji Trophy winner and at one time even a backup for the Indian team.

I tended to keep my distance from the sporty types, especially sports coaches; their hauteur and their height always frightened me. B.P., in particular, was intimidating. He was tall like his daughter, broad and very strong, tanned reddish-brown from the sun, a human brick in a navy blue blazer who strolled about campus with a slow, stately gait, leaving us all bobbing in his wake. Everyone was frightened of him, even the headmaster, even Vikram.

I doubt it was easy for Riya to come to Residency School. I knew she had difficulty making friends, although she didn't really seem to care. When the girls did try to befriend her – especially that teacher's pet Mrinalini, the headmistress' daughter – she was distant and cool, and rarely said much to them beyond a few words. I admired her for what at the time I thought was her independence and self-sufficiency.

The boys were a different matter altogether. I discovered that I wasn't the only one who had fallen for her. This was a problem of supply and demand. Residency School went co-educational in 1980. This was considered progressive by many. Apparently, not by many girls though because for every five boys, we only had one girl. And then there was Riya. The boys talked about her all the time: how short her school skirt was, how she sometimes ran wearing shorts, how when she walked she revealed her thighs, how she sometimes forgot to wear a slip underneath her translucent white shirt. Many boys, especially the seniors, the eleventh- and twelfth-standard boys had a crush on her. They made the juniors from our class slip her notes asking her to meet them after school at the art block, and sent her flowers and boxes of chocolates.

But Riya didn't seem to respond to any of it. She only ever glanced at the chits tucked into her desk, and then threw everything into the dustbin, except the chocolates, which she slipped into her bag.

I saw it all and listened to it, feeling funny on the inside. I didn't want them talking about her, I didn't want anyone but me thinking about her, but I also knew that there was absolutely nothing for me to do except burn silently and invisibly.

10

I WOULD RATHER forget the first encounter I had with her. We had senior school assemblies every day at 8.00 a.m., six days a week, in the damp echoing main hall. The walls were lined with grim portraits of headmasters old and new and the floors with hard wooden benches, only a few with back rests reserved for the seniors. The students – uniformed in white and blue, with a red-and-silver striped tie on every neck – sat in segregated rows of benches, ordered by age. Our small population of orderly clone-like girls, neatly plaited and pleated, occupied the front rows, always staring awkwardly into space, avoiding eye contact with the teachers, keeping their knees tightly joined together, trying to be discreet. The teachers sat lined up on a wooden stage, the women with their tight buns and long-sleeved blouses, the men with their thin moustaches and striped ties; they stared down at us with suspicion and dislike.

I remember being late that day, a few toilets in the dorm had broken down and I had had to wait my turn even as the final bell had rang. The prefect, of course, was not pleased. Sometimes these prefects were scarier than the teachers – like feral animals, hungry for boys to sharpen their fangs on. This one certainly frightened me. He was fierce and muscled, freshly shaven and strongly cologned, and had taken to calling me Oily, referring to the oil that I always put in my hair, a habit hammered into me by my junior school matrons.

And then he shoved me towards my seat amongst the tenth-standard Ashok House boys.

I moved as quickly as I could, which was very slow. I tripped over many legs, whispering apologies to the boys who were softly swearing at me for treading on their feet and bags. Then the prefects hissed at us to be silent as the teachers walked in one by one. I was always struck by how much their hierarchy resembled ours: the senior teachers proudly taking their place in the front rows, the cringing junior teachers wriggling at the back.

'Quiet!' roared Ansari Sir, house master, to no one in particular and the hall suddenly went very still. Though not the most senior, he was the oldest teacher at school and always sat at the coveted spot to the right of the principal.

Just as I reached my seat, everyone rose to their feet. Our mousey, grey-haired principal walked on to the stage, floating in the vermillion Residency School robe which dragged on the ground. The head boy, a very tall muscled sardar who towered over the principal, carried his notes, trailing him.

We all sat down when the principal reached the podium, and he began his morning rant with a prayer. As I settled in for thirty minutes of monotony, I suddenly found myself staring at a head of hair that I knew better than any other in the world.

Riya.

I had previously looked for her in morning assembly, pretending to stretch my back and grabbing quick glances to my left and right. Usually she sat so far away from me that I couldn't see her. But now I found myself right behind her, so close that I could count the wisps of hair on her neck, I could see the outline of her slip under her white shirt, I could reach out and touch her neck.

'Your skirt,' whispered the girl next to her, who had more oil in her hair than I put in mine all week. Riya irritably yanked at the end of her skirt which had ridden up her legs.

I don't know why I did it. I was so close to her I could faintly smell her scent – soap and flowers – but I reached up and gently touched her ponytail, so softly that she did not feel a thing. It felt like the cotton candy I had on the beach one time long ago.

A loud hiss interrupted my thought. Startled, I turned to my right and saw Vikram sitting two boys away, grinning widely and motioning to me. I did not understand what he was saying, until I realized that he wanted me to pull her long hair. I quickly jerked my hand away. It was not my intention to disturb her in any way.

Vikram rolled his eyes, and then bent forward and yanked her ponytail so hard that she yelped loudly right in the middle of the principal's quote of the day. Her voice echoed in the hall, and all three hundred pairs of eyes turned to her. Our principal stopped speaking and trained his small eyes on her. He seemed confused at this unprecedented disruption and his eyes fluttered like dragonflies. Her house prefect, a girl with a hawk nose and thick glasses, gave Riya a furious scowl. There was no doubt that if Riya were a boy, she would have been caned, but I heard that they were not so hard on the girls. Or so I hoped, as I saw the sunken eyes of Deshpande Ma'am – her shrivelled, raisin-like housemistress – bore into her.

I couldn't tell what Riya was thinking or feeling, but she remained as still as a statue, not even turning around to see who had played the dirty trick. Vikram, of course, was grinning like a fool while the boys around him sniggered and patted him on the back.

Suddenly, the boy next to me kicked me hard, and I felt a vice-like grip on my arm. The prefect was staring at me looking very angry.

'On stage, Oily,' he hissed.

There were now three hundred pairs of eyes on me.

I got up as quickly as I could and stumbled towards the stage as the principal droned on. In my daze, I understood that I had won a poetry contest that had been held weeks ago, and now I had to go up on stage and accept the certificate. I remembered vaguely writing a poem called 'A Creature in Love'.

As I came to my senses, I looked in horror at the steps that led up to the stage.

I had accepted awards before, but never here, in this hall. Till the ninth standard the morning assemblies had been held in the sports hall, which doubled as a basketball court. But now I had to face going up at least ten very steep stairs.

As I struggled up the stage as best as I could, taking one step with my good leg, dragging my bad leg behind me, I felt their eyes boring into my back. The whole time though I only thought of her. We were in the same class, but she had never seen me like this, not with my defect on display.

I duly received the award and stumbled off the stage. I walked back to my bench, holding the certificate to my chest, trying my best to disguise my limp. Just before I sat down for just a fraction of a second, I caught her looking at me curiously, and then she gave me what I thought was a faint smile, or maybe it was just a smirk.

I slid back onto the bench wishing I could disappear, and for the rest of the assembly – the morning news and the national anthem – I wondered what she had thought when she had looked at me.

The feeling of embarrassment lasted all day and I berated myself terribly. Why had I let Vikram pull her hair? What had she thought when she saw me climbing up those stairs like an invalid? Why had she smiled at me?

My leg had been crippled for a long time, it was stubby and weak but it had always been as much a part of me as my head and my heart. I never even remembered feeling particularly bad about it – until now. For the first time, I felt utterly short-changed by the universe. Why me? Why was I the only boy with a bad leg? Why couldn't I be like Vikram? Not a champion, I didn't need that, but wasn't it only fair that I should be able to walk and run like other boys.

I skipped games in the afternoon, something I rarely did. Instead, I went back to my dorm and lay down on my small bed. While the rest of the school sprinted and swarmed and galloped across fields, I scalded and burned wishing very hard that I could tear off my dead leg.

11

I HAVE BEEN driving for five hours now. The donkey brown plains have given way to verdant rolling hills. My leg hurts which it rarely does these days. Years of physiotherapy and the country's best doctors had sorted out my problem – or so I had thought.

I pull over, take a sip of water and clean my glasses. I don't know what destructive impulse comes over me, but I take out my phone and Google him. And there he is, on my screen, in my face, an adult Vikram, centre stage even now.

His Facebook page is an ode to himself with a multitude of comments and likes. I zoom into the photograph and he looks curiously the same, the old cosy grin, the puffed-up chest, the full petulant mouth and a newly receding chin. He has lost his thick mane and he is almost bald now, but the baldness suits him somehow.

In one picture, he stands next to a big car; in another, he poses pompously with his father by a large wooden desk, in a third, he shows off a too-thin wife. I scroll down and see articles on his business, on his successes, on his IPO. I see then the obsequious comments of names familiar and new. And then I fall back thirty years.

I wasn't the only one whose circumstances had brought them to Residency School at the age of five. It's strange to think of it now, but Vikram was one of these boys – a teary, sad little mite whose parents had divorced and who kept the rest of us awake at night with his noisy sobs.

In those early years he was undersized, smaller than even

me, and had big round eyes that were often full of tears. He and I were best friends, inseparable, our house matron called us two peas in a pod.

Back then, things were different. I helped him with his schoolwork, and he helped me cope, helping me up stairs, up hills, up ropes in gym class. We spent hours playing marbles, the only game I could enjoy. He shared the imported snacks he always had sent from home. In the third standard, after his father remarried, Vikram told me that he was going home and never coming back. I remember that I begged him to stay, and when he finally left, I cried so much that I was sent to the infirmary for two days.

Four years later, Vikram returned. He was no longer the small sad-eyed boy who played hide-and-seek with me. Now he was tall and arrogant, with long hair he slicked back with gels and white sneakers that looked like rocket launchers compared to the flat-soled canvas shoes that the rest of us wore. When he came back he didn't remember me – or anyone else for that matter. It was as if he had erased the years that he had previously spent at Residency School in the same way I had erased the first five years of my life.

This time around, we did not become friends. His friends were boys on the football team, hockey team and track team. To him, I was just a nerdy guy whose notes he borrowed and who always knew what the right answers were.

There was however one advantageous consequence to our one-time friendship. With so much sweat and testosterone flying around Residency School, there was naturally a lot of bullying, and I presented an almost perfect target: small, weak, crippled. But Vikram – who had very quickly become the unanimous gang leader of our class – and I had an unspoken agreement. He protected me, made sure no one hit or bullied me, and just like in the old days, I helped him with his schoolwork, completing his notebooks, doing his homework, helping him cheat in exams. I don't know why he did this for me. Maybe it was because of those brief years that we had been friends or maybe it was because he realized that he could not survive in this school, just like I could not survive without him.

Later, in biology class I learned that there was a word for this kind of relationship: symbiosis, the interaction between two different organisms from different species living in close physical association – like sea anemones hitchhiking on the backs of hermit crabs, or lactobacillus bacteria living inside human bodies. Vikram and I were like that, two creatures at this school, mutually dependent on one another in order to flourish. He had power over me. But I, in my way, had power over him as well. Little did I know that the minute Riya stepped into our lives everything between us would change.

12

AT RESIDENCY SCHOOL, our schedule was as regimented as a military drill. From Monday through Friday, the first bell went off at 5.00 a.m., then mandatory PT, followed by a hasty breakfast, line-up and morning assembly. Classes began at 8.45 a.m. and went on till 3.30 p.m., after which we had two hours of games. We had evening prep from 6-7.30 p.m., then line-up and dinner. We were meant to 'read quietly' from 8.30 p.m. till lights out at 10.00 p.m. but this was when most boys goofed around or sat glued in front of the TV.

Though Saturdays were only half-days, they seemed to last the longest, and even I, who enjoyed being in class, would find myself watching the clock, the seconds moving like minutes, the minutes like hours. The classrooms would fill with the irritation and impatience that radiated from us like fumes, the boys wanting to run onto their respective fields, the girls I wasn't sure what they did, but I knew that Riya, like the boys, went straight to the tracks.

One Saturday stands out in my memory as the most important Saturday in my life. We were playing Daly College in the finals of the IPSC cup, and even I knew this was an important match. Everyone was more wound up than usual, particularly during the last period, Rao Ma'am's maths class.

Rao Ma'am was indisputably my least favourite teacher. She was small and wicked and always wore high, pointed heels. Even though I loved maths, her class was boring – I was studying calculus, while the rest of the class was still on trigonometry and all throughout her class I had to feign interest.

Exam season was when Rao Ma'am came into her own. She was a notoriously difficult marker, and had a cruel style of announcing our results to the class – but only at the end of the lesson.

This particular Saturday signified the return of our first mid-term examination. Throughout the class she wistfully cradled and stroked the stack of white examination papers as though it were a beloved pet, while all of us sat on tenterhooks. It wasn't uncommon for students, especially the girls, to cry or to faint during the announcement of these marks. Even I, who hardly ever got below a 90 per cent, was experiencing great stress. I could not imagine what it must be like for the others, especially Riya, who often had amongst the lowest marks in class.

As Rao Ma'am started her charade, I held my breath and closed my eyes.

'Nikhil, ninety-five. Very good,' she said in a bored drawl. I exhaled in relief.

Vikram had a fifty-six. 'Scope for improvement,' commented Rao Ma'am wryly.

Vikram sauntered to the front of the class, retrieved his paper and patted me heartily on the shoulder as he slipped back to his desk. I hoped Rao Ma'am hadn't noticed – I had passed him chits throughout the exam.

Mrinalini had scored a ninety-five as well. She was the only one in class who posed any sort of real competition to me.

'Wonderful,' said Rao Ma'am with a smile.

The simpering Mrinalini walked back to her desk, a smug grin on her face. Most teachers loved the goody-two-shoes Mrinalini, but I found her annoying and conniving. She always copied my notes; when I had asked her only once to give me hers she had refused.

I waited for Riya's results, holding my breath for so long that I started seeing stars. The truth was that I was more nervous for her than I had been for myself. I stole a glance at her; she was doodling on the back of her mathematics notebook, she didn't seem concerned at all.

Rao Ma'am's voice cracked like a rime of ice. 'Riya. Thirty-five. The lowest in the class.'

Riya walked up to the front of the class in her usual

confident lope, her heavy blue skirt swinging around her knees, a slightly embarrassed look on her face.

'Sorry, Ma'am,' she said, though she didn't seem sorry at all, and turned around to walk back to her seat.

Just when Riya was about to sit down, Rao Ma'am said, 'Riya, come outside with me.'

The bell rang just then, signalling the end of the week.

Riya didn't know that I was still in the classroom when she returned. I was sitting at the back, behind a tangle of desks and chairs, completing my homework so I could spend my Sunday reading Ruskin Bond's new book. Everyone else had left to watch the football match and I could already hear the cheers erupting like war cries.

She walked to her desk, but instead of carelessly throwing a few books into her bag like she usually did, she remained standing. After a moment, she sat down heavily on the hard wooden chair and put her head in her arms on the table, her ponytail spilling messily everywhere.

At first, I didn't hear her, but then the throaty, painful sounds became apparent. I had been in boarding school long enough to decipher the sound of a concealed sob. I sat very still, aware that I was intruding on her and her tears.

Finally she got up, sniffled twice, and brushed her hair out of her face. She opened her desk, grabbed her empty backpack and stalked out of the classroom. I don't know why I did it, but I followed her out.

Despite my bad leg, I walked pretty fast, and I saw that she was heading in the direction of the tracks. I followed her past the academic block, past the main building, and across the vast cricket field, till finally I reached the red-sand tracks at the edge of the campus next to Scindia Pavilion.

By the time I arrived, she had already changed, and she was in her sports uniform: a white-collared sports shirt and a navy divided skirt. She sat on the track, putting her spikes on, while I stood a safe distance away, concealed by a large rhododendron bush.

She got up, brushed the sand off her legs, and went to the chalked starting line. She crouched low, the tips of her fingers on the ground, her knees slightly bent. She lowered her head, paused for a moment, and suddenly pushed off.

I had watched people running my whole life, but I had never seen anything like this. Most people, even the fast ones, pound with their feet, turning red in their face, sweating like pigs, making running look like hard work. But not Riya. She ran so swiftly, so gracefully, that she seemed to be gliding on air. She ran like a dancer, every part of her body – her arms, her legs, her head, her chest – moved separately, yet they seemed to be one. Lost in her rhythm, she seemed transformed. No longer the haughty girl with the cold, blank stare in her eyes who didn't speak with anyone. That was some sort of a pretence to fool people like me. She seemed now to be someone else, someone happy and content and free.

13

RIYA WAS SO bad at mathematics that Rao Ma'am was making us study partners with immediate effect. This essentially meant that she would study while I would explain things to her; I was more or less an unpaid tutor. The strict

Rao Ma'am only appointed co-ed study partners in the most dire circumstances. This situation qualified because Riya had failed the last three maths exams.

And so Riya and I finally spoke for the first time three months after she had walked into my life.

I waited for her in an empty classroom in the ninth-standard building in the academic block. It was evening and the smells of winter lingered in the air: wood smoke and pine and damp leaves. Dusk was falling now, earlier than usual, and by the time she arrived, ten minutes late, it was already dark. She sauntered in wearing her sports uniform with an oversize dark blue sweater that covered half of her blue skirt. Her face was tinged with pink and her knees were streaked with dirt. She smelled of iron and grass, her hair was tied into a loose, messy bun that threatened to come tumbling down with the smallest shake of her head. It appeared that she had come straight from the track.

I was relieved when I saw her. I had set up thirty minutes in advance and had been staring at the hands of the clock, convinced that she would never come. But now that she was here, I was so nervous I could hardly speak. I had watched her and learned about her and worshipped her. But I had never actually spoken with her, not once in the three months she had been at the school. She, on the other hand, just looked annoyed. I saw that she had brought nothing with her but her spikes.

'You're my tutor,' she said sceptically.

I looked up at her and then quickly dropped my gaze. 'Nikhil,' I said, muttering into my book.

'I know,' she said, leaning forward to tie her shoe. 'We're in the same class.'

We sat in silence for a long moment and I suddenly realized I had no idea what I was supposed to do. Algebra, arithmetic, nothing seemed to add up. Worst of all, I couldn't even speak, so we just sat there in an uncomfortable silence, the shrill cries of an animal somewhere wafting in through the windows.

She finally broke the tension. 'Where do we start?' she asked in a bored drawl.

I flipped the pages of my notebook, cleared my throat and stuttered, 'Where, uh, do you want to start?'

'I thought you were the smart one.'

My voice seemed stuck in my throat. I made a small choking noise. She looked at me in a strange way. Then she spoke again, but gently this time, 'I guess we should start from the beginning.'

'The beginning,' I said, 'would be good.'

14

IN THE BEGINNING, no matter how hard I tried, I couldn't get her attention. I didn't blame her completely. I too was an absolute mess; my lessons were wildly disorganized, I stuttered and stammered stupidly forgetting even the most basic of concepts and then I would go off on nonsensical rants as she stared at me without any clue or interest. Once, I was so nervous that I clutched my pencil so tightly it broke in my hand. Now she probably thought that I was not only a geek, but also very strange. She, I remembered, had been looking especially pretty that day.

The truth was that she was really not very good at mathematics. She was hopeless in geometry, and could not find X to save her life. She could not be bothered about probabilities, and my carefully constructed rate questions – posed always in running terms to generate her interest – always fell flat.

Gradually though things improved when I realized that instead of trying to teach her what I knew, I had to find some sort of common mathematical ground. So I began with the basics and the more I taught, the more confident I became. Finally, a breakthrough came during a class on polynomials when I realized with a start that she was actually paying attention.

After my explanation I gave her a sum to try her hand at.

'This one is easy.'

'It is?' I said, thrilled that she thought so and even happier when I saw that she had got the simple sum correct.

'Give me another,' she said, sitting up a little straighter, a hint of a challenge now in her voice.

'Really?' I said, surprised. Normally she made me solve all the sums that I gave her.

'Yeah, this is kind of fun.'

'All right then.' I quickly jotted down another sum before she changed her mind.

She pondered over the equation for a few minutes and then scribbled her answer on the page.

'I got this,' she said brightly.

'Let's take a look,' I said in my authoritative best.

I looked at the chequered page of her mathematics notebook and there in her messy handwriting she had solved the sum perfectly in just three steps, while I, her teacher, had taken five.

And then looking at me, smiling fondly, she said, 'This one was too easy, give me the next.'

It was the first time Riya surprised me. It would not be the last.

Despite her poor marks, I realized that Riya was very intelligent. When she focused, she grasped concepts quickly, and sometimes she asked questions so pointed that they confused even me. Riya's moods, I discovered, depended on her running. When she ran well, she worked hard in class, applying herself, trying to understand why sinA=cosA=1. When she hadn't run well, she was dark, staring stormily at sums, sighing, chewing her pen to bits.

I also discovered that she had almost no fundamentals. This was the reason she looked blankly at the blackboard so often: she had no clue what was going on in class. She admitted that over the past few years, she had missed a lot of school. She was often away for long stretches of time for district, state or national track meets, and in her previous school they had passed her even when she got very poor marks because she was a star athlete. At Residency School, although sports were all-important, you couldn't just fail or miss school. You had to pass with decent marks, or cheat effectively like Vikram and his friends. When I had hinted at this option, she had just looked at me as if I were a fool.

It was uncommon for kids to switch schools in the tenth standard, the year of the board exams, and I had a strong feeling that if Riya hadn't come to Residency School, she would have just failed the national board exam.

But now that I had come into her life, I was determined to change all of that.

And though we didn't have much in common – I liked books, she liked to run, I liked maths, she liked to run. I liked studying, and she … she liked to run, but somehow with numbers, formulae and equations egging us on, Riya and I slowly became friends.

15

RIYA MADE A face, squinting at her notes. 'Specs, your sum is wrong.'

She called me Specs, short for the spectacles I wore.

'My name is *Nikhil*,' I replied. 'The sum is *right*, your answer is not. And I can't understand your handwriting.'

I always thought that neat, flowery handwriting came naturally to girls. But Riya scribbled like a boy, her handwriting as messy as mine was neat. I was convinced that teachers just sloshed red ink on her notebooks because they couldn't understand a thing she wrote.

I had suggested, very seriously, that maybe she should go back to those cursive writing books of our childhood, but she had just cocked one eyebrow and laughed out loud.

'You're crazy, Specs! My handwriting is fine. You just need to get your eyes checked.'

So often, I just did not have an answer to the things she said.

'You know that I am doing you a *favour* by teaching you, right?' I managed to retort, after a pause that went on slightly too long.

'You're a teacher's pet, aren't you, Specs?' she teased.

Sometimes I had to remind her who was in charge.

'No, Riya, I'm just trying to help you out. Rao Ma'am sometimes asks me to help weak students out.'

'I'm not a weak student,' she said loftily.

'You got a *two* in your last maths exam. Out of hundred.'

That seemed to shut her up and we got down to work.

And in the weeks that followed, from two she went to twelve, then twenty-four, then thirty-six and then finally fifty marks, where she staked her claim and stayed solidly put.

16

OVER TUITIONS SHE slowly opened up to me. Riya was B.P.'s only child, her mother had passed away when she was young. She had not much liked her last school in New Delhi, but she said she had tolerated it mostly because she was hardly ever there. The more I got to know her, the more I realized how little she liked it at Residency School. It was the small things … the way she sat listlessly through classes. The way she ignored most people. The way, after the final bell rang, she never spent even an extra second after class, but ran away straight to the tracks.

It seemed to me that Riya genuinely didn't care what people thought. To her it was a matter of complete indifference that the girls didn't accept her, or that the boys thought her bold. While I found this refreshing, others did not. Mrinalini, the insufferable busybody, snubbed by Riya, rallied the girls against her, till even the most benign girls wouldn't say a word to her. When it became known that I was Riya's tutor, and her friend, boys approached me to put in a good word for them. Regrettably, the matter even came to Vikram's attention, despite my efforts to keep it quiet, and, by extension, protect her.

Vikram was a skilled bully, as deft with cruelty as he was with his hockey stick. Like most predators, he always selected the most vulnerable of the herd. Thanks to our arrangement, he generally let me be. I liked to think that perhaps I was his weakness, a reminder of the way he used to be, so long ago. As a matter of principle, Vikram typically left girls alone, maybe because they were too easy, not enough sport. This changed, however, when he met Riya. I do not know what set them off, but they despised one another, right away. I figured it was because she, unlike most people, wasn't afraid of him.

Vikram would slouch in the back of the classroom and make snide remarks. Riya would snap back. Most of the girls complied with the Residency School's unspoken rules: you tolerate a boy's teasing and, if need be, you cry silently into your handkerchief. But not her. She would whirl around, letting loose a barrage of curses, which would impress even the boys.

The war continued in the halls, at breaks, in the dorms, becoming a famous contest of wills. The whole class eagerly followed each episode, Vikram's latest atrocity, Riya's most recent defiance. I hated it the whole time, hinting to her during our tuitions to make peace with him. But she just looked at me with fiery eyes. I had known Vikram for many years, and I knew that when he wanted to win, it was impossible for anyone, even for Riya, to beat him. The worst of it was when Vikram got his friends involved. They would whistle and hiss when she walked into class, make comments on the length of her skirt, about her ponytail and about how she wore shorts while she ran.

It gradually wore Riya down. I saw how she pretended to do schoolwork during tea break, sometimes even skipping tea completely, so that she would not have to have tea by herself. I noticed how she lingered in the classroom when the lunch bell rang, waiting for everyone else to walk out in their groups, so she didn't have to walk alone. When it was time for games, she ran out of the class, so she didn't have to be the only one packing her bag silently while everyone else chatted about the day that had passed.

During these times, I desperately wished that I could have given her company; snuck her a biscuit and a cup of tea, walk with her to lunch, or stand by her desk while she packed her bag. After all, she and I were friends and wasn't that what friends did? But this sort of behaviour wasn't allowed in our school – at least not between boys and girls in tenth grade. If you were even *seen* talking with a girl, just the two of you, you were teased, rejected, possibly thrashed. So, I stayed away from her during class and in the halls, between periods, after supper. I taught her math, I watched her from the corner of my eye, wishing that I could be with her. Maybe she thought my behaviour was strange, but I figured that by now she knew how it went at Residency School, so she and I both stuck to the unwritten rules.

17

AS I WALKED alone down the cobblestone paths, I knew that winter had finally set in. The air was damp and misty, the greenery of the conifer trees was giving way to brown. Usually, I hated the onset of winter. The new cold made my leg hurt, and when it snowed, I could scarcely get around campus. This winter though was better than it had ever been before. Everything, even the unpleasant things, somehow seemed magical and romantic – the icy cold air that burnt my chest; the dark winter nights that came around sometimes as early as 4.00 p.m.; even the cold dampness that hung in the air.

Today, she had been in a good mood and though we hadn't studied much, she told me about the race that she had just run.

'She came in at the bend and she tried to trip me. Imagine that! What a lowlife technique,' Riya beamed. 'But, I slowed down so suddenly that she actually fell and she took down two stragglers with her too.'

Her hair shook as she laughed. I listened quietly, wondering – as I always did whenever she talked about her races – what it would be like to actually run.

Riya was my laughter and lightness, my fun, my silliness, and I looked forward to our hour together more than anything else.

When I arrived at the dorm after spending a blissful hour with her, the sour smell of post-games sweat and socks hit me. I wished for the thousandth time that next year, in eleventh grade, I would be placed in a room with someone like me, a non-athlete, a science student, though we were a rare specimen at the school.

I walked over to my bed, the last in a row of fifteen tucked into a dark, dank corner which no one had wanted to have, and lay down for a few minutes recalling moments of the day, how her skirt had gathered in little pleats around her brown thighs, and how she had scratched the tip of her nose with the end of her pen.

I hardly heard them walk in; lulled by the cold, I was sinking into a gentle sleep. My last hazy thought was that they would probably drop clumps of mud everywhere that I would have to clean up later.

I woke up with a start when I felt a wet blob on my face. Even before I reached out and touched it, I knew that it was somebody's spit. I opened my eyes and there were twelve jeering faces looking down at me. Amongst them was Vikram, his big white teeth stretched into a wolfish sneer.

I reached for my glasses, but within seconds one of the boys grabbed them and placed them on his nose. He shrieked out in alarm at the high power, and then everyone laughed.

'How were tuitions?' asked Vikram, in a cold and clear voice.

'F-ff-ine,' I stuttered, holding the fear at bay.

'Do anything besides geometry?' said one of the boys.

I couldn't tell exactly who was speaking, I didn't have my glasses on. A part of me was glad, because I had thought that some of the boys in Vikram's gang were my friends. I suddenly heard an unforgiving crunch. *My glasses*, I thought with horror. I couldn't afford another pair. Someone grabbed my arm and twisted it behind my head. I grimaced with pain and looked at Vikram. Why was he behaving this way? I simply didn't understand. I had just finished a science project for him that had saved him from failing the class.

And then I heard his voice, hard as a rock.

'Oily, this here is a bottle of ink, an objects nerds like you know very well.'

I heard a few sniggers and squirmed uncomfortably, trying without luck to readjust my arm, which was now in excruciating pain.

'We need you to dump this whole thing inside Riya Pratap's desk.'

On hearing her name, I no longer felt a thing in my arm.

'Riya?' I dumbly said.

'*Riya.* You remember her, don't you? The bitch you sniff around.'

'But … her copies…' I muttered under my breath.

His voice was soft and dangerous. 'Yes, Oily. That's exactly the point. Dump this *inside* her desk on *top* of her copies. And bring us back a few copies too.'

A bottle of indigo ink landed hard on top of my knee. 'But … the boards…' I squeaked.

But they didn't seem to hear me, my voice was drowned out by their howling laugh.

Vikram's goon let go of my arm and he stomped away with the rest of them.

I stared after them as they walked away, and then suddenly Vikram turned around, a vicious look on his face.

'If I were you, I would make sure I do this and bring back those copies too,' he said in a dangerous tone.

With jeers they walked out of the room, swinging their hockey sticks like swords.

I couldn't sleep that night. Every time one of the boys got up to go to the loo, I thought it was someone coming over to beat me up with a hockey stick or to pour ink all over me.

For most of my life, Vikram had protected me in lieu of help with schoolwork. So, unlike most boarding school boys, who had gone through some bullying at least, I hadn't been bullied much at all and so now I was scared out of my wits.

What would they do to me? Beat me till I bled? Kick me till parts of me were as blue as the bottles of ink that lay at my side? Break parts of my body? What if they did something to my leg?

More than anything I wondered why Vikram was doing this. It wasn't like he was my friend but with the boards around the corner I figured he could use my help now more than anytime else. In a sense, I was a valuable person. He needed me. But maybe that had changed. Perhaps he'd found another helper – Mrinalini? – or he had a contingency plan. Maybe he counted me being so weak that he could do this, and still expect my assistance. But still, what had I ever done to deserve this? I couldn't get my head around it and thoughts buzzed in my mind like stinging bees.

Going to the teachers was not an option, not if I were to have any sort of future in this school. The last boy to do that, back when I was in the sixth standard, had been tormented so cruelly that he voluntarily left the school. If I did not do what they asked me to, I feared what they would do to me. But the thought of doing what they wanted me to do was even more devastating.

Stealing notebooks and pouring ink may seem like a trivial act, but with the board exams around the corner, these notebooks were our lifelines. We had spent all year working on them, so that we could use these to study for our boards. These notebooks were as precious as jewels. I of all people knew this well. I kept mine guarded in the cabinet beneath my bed with a heavy-duty lock, because they were always the first ones to get nicked.

If I besmirched her copies with ink, how would she study? What would she do? What if I told them I did it, but never did? They would probably find that out, after all we spent all day in class. How would I possibly get away from that?

And Riya, what if she found out what I had done? Would I lose her forever? Would she ever speak to me again? Every permutation and combination had a disastrous solution, and I knew that there was no simple way out.

I tossed and turned all night till finally at dawn I fell into a fitful sleep, awoken a few hours later by the screeching final morning bell. I struggled into my uniform without even brushing my teeth, my leg still hurting like hell.

All through the day, the only thing I could think about was them coming at me with hockey sticks, like I had seen them do with other boys, me lying in a corner, blood spewing out of my face. The sight of Riya usually made everything better, but today I couldn't bear looking at her. I was too exhausted by the end of the day to even walk. During our mandatory games period, when I was meant to 'walk and run', I must have looked so bad that the coach told me to go rest. I slunk off beneath a banyan tree and lay on the cool grass, looking up at the brown-bottomed clouds gathering menacingly on the horizon beneath a royal blue sky. Behind me, a crow, perched on a leafy oleander bush, lifted noisily into the sky; only if I were like that crow and could fly far away, too but I was stuck here, earthbound with my problems. Forget about flying, I couldn't even run.

The next day when Vikram and his goons began warning me, tapping their hockey sticks and cricket bats menacingly on the ground, I realized that I had no choice. I would have to spill the blue ink inside her desk and steal her notebooks. But I decided that I would also make amends. I could not leave Riya without her notes, not now, not when she had come such a long way. I would make fresh notes for her, of every single subject that I could. Photocopying was not an option, as I did not have enough money for that expensive process, so I would copy all the notebooks myself. They wouldn't be her notes, written by her hand; but sometimes I doubted that she could even understand her own writing, like ants crawling around on the page. It would take me hours and hours – I would have to copy during meals, during classes, during break, during prep, but no matter, it would be a small price to pay for what I would do to her. I only hoped that she would never ever find out that I had spilt the ink, or that I had stolen her notebooks, because that I knew I would simply never be able to bear.

18

I SNUCK INTO the classroom after games while everyone was at tea, my heart flapping like the wings of an injured bird. I had with me the two bottles of ink, expensive Parker ink that I couldn't afford to use, yet Vikram could buy for a ruthless prank.

Thankfully Riya did not use a lock on her desk. I guess she didn't have much to protect.

My hands were shaking badly and little tremors of fear were rising through my spine, but I managed to lift the top of her wooden desk. The inside of her desk was messy – notebooks thrown carelessly in, bits of paper floating around, carcasses of pens, pencil shavings, a few hair ties, and an old pair of socks, that for a second I thought of stealing for myself, but then the bell rang, and I realized with a jolt that I had much less time than I had previously thought.

Hurriedly, I searched for the notebooks I had decided to steal, English, economics, civics – the easier subjects. I was so nervous that I was spilling the ink even when I didn't intend to and the fear was choking my breath. Everything was taking much longer than expected. It didn't help that her desk was disorganized and so many of her notebooks were unlabelled and then of course there was the matter of her messy handwriting, which, after all this time, I still didn't quite understand.

I had been in there almost ten minutes, and tea break was about to end. The warning bell had already rung, after which some students would come in to get the books they had left behind. I was so frightened now that I just wanted to dump the ink and bolt, but I had planned to spill the ink strategically so that it wouldn't ruin all her notebooks. But now I could not move, I could not think, I just stood there frozen in fear like a fool.

And then I heard the unmistakable clip of high heels on the marble floors.

Some survival instinct greater than fear took over me and I acted so quickly that even my brain didn't comprehend. It was as if some survival instinct greater than fear took over me and endowed me with superhuman speed. I grabbed a few notebooks, dumped the ink and slammed the desk shut. But I couldn't move fast enough, my leg had no life, but it did have a mind of its own.

The irascible Rao Ma'am walked in and saw me standing next to Riya's desk. Rao Ma'am: my nemesis, my albatross, my saviour for assigning me my Riya. Her face was dangerously still, her eyes unnaturally hard. For a long moment she clocked the mess by my side, scraps of paper, her notebooks, the ink, even her socks. She pursed her lips and pointed a talon-like finger at me as I stood there, notebook in my hand, my heart racing, guilt written in red on my face.

'You,' she said sharply. 'You're in trouble, young man.'

19

AS EXPECTED, RAO Ma'am immediately reported me to Ansari Sir, who was almost as much at a loss of words as I.

I was the quiet one, the good one. The one who had never once given any teacher trouble, who could be relied on to tutor others, but now here I was vandalizing property and stealing notebooks.

Ansari Sir was as strict as he was old and he had a knack for making boys cry, regularly beating them with the cane with which he walked.

I stood there in silence, hands clasped behind my back, my skinny legs shaking like twigs in a storm.

Ansari Sir leaned back in his chair and fixed his ancient watery, red-rimmed eyes on me.

Finally, I stammered, 'So-oorry, sir.'

Ansari Sir leaned forward and cleared his throat, then in his pseudo British accent, far too British to be genuinely British, said, 'And what were you doing when Rao Ma'am found you?'

Although, I had planned the operation a hundred times, I had never once thought of what I would say if I got caught, that thought had simply not occurred to me.

'Sir,' I finally mumbled. 'I … I was confused.'

'Confused?' he said so loudly that his jowls quivered.

'Sir … I, sir, I don't know, I thought that maybe this…'

He cut me off. Guilt was pumping off me. I sounded like the liar and thief that I was.

'This is no time to be doing this. No time to be stealing things. Right before the boards. If I report this to the principal, both you and your scholarship will be in big trouble.'

'Sir, I wasn't stealing,' I said with a squeak.

'That's for Miss Pratap to answer,' he said coolly.

Then without another word, he brought out a ruler from his desk, and, with his gnarled, veiny hands, he begin thrashing me with unbelievable speed, hitting my palms so hard that the metal ruler turned red.

20

EVERYONE KNEW WHAT had happened to me, but no one said a word. Beatings were a relatively common occurrence at Residency School and red swollen palms were almost a badge of pride. But to me they were a mark of shame.

In class the next day, there was a lot of commotion when Riya, rifling through her desk, held up ink-stained notebooks.

Vikram smiled and saluted me sarcastically. Mrinalini rushed over to attempt to console her. I cowed in my seat, too ashamed to look at her while the rest of them just howled with laughter and whistled through their teeth.

I was awake that night and several other nights after. I was either up completing notes for Riya, or I was too disturbed to sleep. I despised myself for what I had done, for being such a spineless, pathetic fool.

In many ways, the notes were a saving grace. They kept me sane as mortifying thoughts flooded my mind. Would they send me back home? Take away my scholarship? Now that my grandfather was dead, my grandmother would never be able to afford to pay for this expensive school. The worst thoughts visited me just as I would finally fall asleep. Did she know? What if she found out? Would she ever speak with me again?

If she knew what I had done, she never let me know, and

as difficult as it was for me to face her, our tuitions continued, mostly because I realized how important these lessons were for her. I owed her that much, and more.

Riya, noticing me tired and nervous, and even getting sums wrong, asked me more and more often if I was all right – even acting more cheerful than usual, as though to allay my guilt.

'You got something wrong. Something must be wrong with your specs,' she teased.

The absolute truth was that I really couldn't see. I was wearing a five-year-old pair of glasses with the wrong power. But, this trouble paled in comparison to the others I had right now.

'What happened to your hands?' she asked curiously once, lightly touching the broad welt with her finger. It was the first time she had ever touched me.

I pulled back and cleared my throat.

'Polynomials. Many-sided shapes. Ever heard of them?'

Days passed by and nothing happened and no one said a word. I got more and more scared. Ansari Sir ignored me like he mostly did. Rao Ma'am went back to her old habit of asking for my copies to check the other students' homework. After the prank, Vikram and his gang left me alone. Strangely, they also left Riya alone: no more teasing or harassing, the war, evidently, had ended. Perhaps Vikram had grown bored or maybe he was behaving this way out of pity, so that my last days could be pleasant, the same way jailers were kind to prisoners about to be hanged.

Then finally, six days after Rao Ma'am had reported me, Ansari Sir called me in.

This time, I was mentally prepared. I had promised myself

that no matter what happened, I would go with dignity and maintain some self-respect. I would try to be a man, there would be absolutely no crying, no matter what.

Ansari Sir, leafing through a book, didn't even look up at me when I came in.

I stood in front of his big wooden desk, eyes on the floor, my chin to my chest, my hands clasped behind my back, the portraits of ex-Ashok House headmasters staring at me stiffly from their places on the wall. They would smile, I knew, when my sentence was given to me. The acid yellow light of the uncovered tube light made Ansari Sir's pale skin seem almost green.

He spoke sharply, it sounded like a ruler cracking and I flinched. 'Physics copy up to date?'

'Yes, sir,' I bleated like a lamb.

'Drop it off after dinner then.'

Teachers often asked me for my impeccable notebooks, which were sometimes even better than their own. I stood there in silence, closing my eyes, waiting for him to drop the bomb. A couple of seconds later and all I heard was the unsteady scratching of his pen. I opened my eyes and he looked up sharply at me.

'That will be all,' he said irritably, and waved me out with his hand.

I turned around, utterly confused. And just as I was about to shut his heavy oak door, he spoke again:

'And about that matter.'

For a moment, I felt as if I may have a heart attack. 'Sir.'

'Miss Pratap said that nothing was amiss. I suggest you have your eyes checked and glasses changed in time for the boards.'

21

THE HAND-OFF WENT better than I had expected, she accepted the notes I had made for her without a word, and then just walked away. If she had known that I had done this or wondered why I had, she did not say and she did not ask. I thought about it for years afterwards. What and how much did she really know? It seemed impossible to me that she could not have suspected what had passed, but if she had, why hadn't she ever asked?

Luckily, there wasn't much time for me to dwell on the incident, because the tenth-grade board exams had arrived and for the first time in many lives, academics took centre stage. All the cricketers, footballers and hockey players were forced to dig up their half-empty notebooks and desperately try to learn a year's worth of studies in a matter of days. I, of course, was very well prepared.

Cheating was an important aspect of academic life at Residency School. Peons were bribed to smuggle out papers from teachers' offices, questions were leaked, and rich boys like Vikram took paid tuitions from junior teachers, tipping them generously to give them some of the questions that would appear in the exams. All sorts of tactics were employed – chits were snuck into all parts of the body, and then swallowed like a piece of chewing gum once the cheater had seen what he had to see, to erase all trace of his crime. Boys devised complex codes and signals to communicate during the exams. I often thought that if this much effort was applied to studying, students would pass with flying colours. Despite all these creative efforts, so many failed and the teachers had to pass them by giving them grace marks, especially if they were athletes. This just went to show the glorious standards of our school.

But the board exams were a national examination, and the Residency School's code of conduct did not hold. There would be external exam papers, external examiners and external markers, and our school's most experienced cheaters knew that there was little they could do. It was close to impossible to 'manage' these exams, even for those whose connections ran far and deep.

I usually became popular during exam time, but during the boards, I experienced popularity like never before. My perfect notebooks were hugely in demand and some of the athletes, whom I had boarded with for years, had learned that I had tutored Riya successfully; as a consequence, many came looking for me, their big heads hanging from their thick necks, gruffly requesting my help.

It began with a few cricketers. Then the word spread, and soon I had a full classroom of sportsmen and athletes staring dumbly at the blackboard. I was shocked to discover that many of my tutees could not even manage eighth-standard material. They had trouble balancing a simple equation, let alone solve a quadratic equation. Some of them couldn't even do long division, let alone trigonometry. One poor boy couldn't even tell the x-axis from the y.

At first I was hesitant to tutor them. I had my own studying – and Riya – to think about. But could I really say no? Everyone in the hostel was so high strung that I feared that they would beat me up if I refused. Also, I learnt from my experience with Riya that the best way of mastering the subject was to teach someone else.

So I began teaching group classes. And just like my experience with Riya, at first I was nervous, but then I got in the groove. I had never had so many people who actually listened to me, and now here were the most celebrated boys in school, struggling to hold on to my every word, staring at me wide-eyed, copying every word that I wrote on the board. All of this stirred feelings of vanity and pride in me that I had never known.

I cannot lie. It felt really good and I got wrapped up in it, planning lessons, even giving mini-exams. Maybe this is what boys felt when they were leading teams or shouting out commands; why so many boys competed to become captain of this or that, to feel like the way I was feeling right now.

This was the first time that I had so many friends, if you could call them that. I knew enough about the Residency School boys to realize that they were only 'friends' with me because they needed something – but still it was nice to have people sitting down next to me during meals, not because it was the only free seat, but because I was sitting there. It was pleasant to have boys thumping your back, though sometimes they did it so hard that I tripped. It felt good to be part of frivolous, jokey conversations during showers and before bed, even though I hardly cared about what they said.

I became so well-liked during this time that even if Vikram had wanted to bully me, he wouldn't have been able to touch me. I had my own personal army of muscle-head tutees, whose tenure at Residency School depended on me.

Despite all this, Riya remained my priority, far more than even my own studies. I was terrified at the prospect of her failing. I had recurring nightmares about it: exam sheets drenched in vermillion, report cards splattered with red ink. Worst of all was one particular scene that ran through my head – Riya taking an exam, her pen in her mouth, staring out of the window in that blank way of hers because she knew nothing at all.

The situation at our school became frenzied as the board exams approached. Cartons of sugary soft-drinks were shipped in to help boys stay awake, and the hospital became packed with students who had consumed too much coffee or tea and developed gastritis. Irritable athletes, used to endorphin kicks but now chained to their desks, kept on getting into brawls. Two boys ended up with broken ribcages, another two with broken noses. The girls, it was believed, were handling the exam stress better than the boys, although I heard a rumour that Mrinalini and her main rival were caught in a fight so bad that both ended up with bald spots where they had pulled out each other's hair.

What made it all worse is that we were having the coldest winter ever in the hundred-and two-year history of the school. It was so cold that it would not even snow and the lawns glittered with frost every morning. The distant mountain ranges, always shrouded by warm clouds, became jagged and crystalline, rising up like the sharp graphs that gave my unfortunate students such a difficult time. Athletes who had no trouble playing sports in sub-zero winters – often in heaps of snow – bleated miserably that they found it impossible to study in the cold and often made huge fires of used rough notebooks to keep themselves warm. The few heaters that our house owned became the subject of so much fighting that eventually all of them broke.

The cold made it harder for me too, simply because my leg hurt a lot more. Except for my daily trip to tutor Riya, I generally stayed in the hostel, studying or teaching. That said, I didn't mind the long hours in the hostel, because people were so nice to me. Seeing me limping around, the muscle heads offered up their vast repertoire of hot packs, unguents and ointments, and so like this I got through the winter better than ever before.

22

THREE DAYS BEFORE our first board exam, which to my greatest fear was maths, I tutored Riya well past our daily hour.

She was distracted and nervous these days. While it was normal for her to be distracted, it wasn't at all like her to be nervous about anything. But the board exams were important, and she knew the consequences would be dire if she failed. It didn't help that every time she made a mistake I became visibly distraught, so much so that I had to take off my glasses and rub my eyes. I was glad at least that she couldn't look inside my head and see what was happening there.

But today had been a better day. She had walked in looking so pretty, wisps of her hair flying in the air, her eyes round and bright, a small smile playing on her lips and even though there was nothing different about her than any other day, she seemed to be lighter, happier, like she was somewhere else in her mind. I guessed on a track somewhere. This also meant that she wasn't listening to a single word that I said.

As I derived Pythagoras's theorem vigorously, Riya just sat there, dreamily masticating the end of her pen with her mouth, her dimpled chin resting in the cup of her hand, not even pretending to pay attention to what was a sure-shot board exam question.

I couldn't help but be annoyed at her.

I looked at her with what I considered a fierce look, which I had tested on the muscle heads to great effect.

'The maths exam is only three days away. You should know how to do this.'

Riya just looked at me, smiled and swivelled her head away. That girl, she knew exactly how to get under my skin. Then she got up, pirouetted on her feet and skipped to the blackboard.

She drew a triangle on the board and set out to prove the theorem. Hawk-like I followed each step with my eyes.

'Is this what I should know?' she asked, stopping mid-theorem, turning around and studying me for a moment, looking me straight in the eye.

I frowned. 'It's not finished yet.'

'And how do I finish it?'

I sat down on the edge of a desk, looked at the board and then at her.

I had taught her this a hundred times. How did she not know the next step?

I tried to keep my voice from shaking. I was angry at her, nervous for her, scared that she would fail.

I pushed my glasses up my nose.

'Take it step by step,' I said slowly.

Instead of solving the problem on the board, she turned around and then out of nowhere, as if it was the most natural thing in the world, in the sweetest, gentlest tone that I had ever heard from her, she said, 'You know, Specs, I like you more than I ever thought I would.'

I sat there unblinking, my heart doing a somersault in my chest. And then the unthinkable happened. I stared at the board, mixing up all the angles and lines till Pythagoras's theorem, which I could derive in the deepest of my sleep, made no sense at all.

'Is that … uh … a compliment?' I blurted out the only thing that came to me, though so many thoughts were swirling through my head.

She sighed, gave me a sideways look and then turned back to the blackboard.

'Specs, for how smart you are at your books, sometimes I think you are really dumb.'

With that, her heavy skirt flying in the air, she turned her back on me and walked away, taking my jittery heart with her wherever she went.

I sat there for some time in the empty classroom, my heart beating abnormally fast, feeling warm though it was very cold. After a while, I got up, gathered my things and walked towards the door. That's when I noticed the hasty scribbling on the board. Now that I had my senses back I saw that every step of her messily derived Pythagoras's theorem was perfectly correct.

23

DRIVING UP THE circuitous mountain road, I cross a village and stop for a moment to check my email. But my phone has no reception, so I stand by my car, watching some bedraggled, dirt-smeared children playing a game with twigs and a plastic ball. I can't help but smile, they seem to be thoroughly enjoying themselves. There is absolute freedom in their screams, their movements, in their laughter, even in this game that they are playing with seemingly no rules.

I think then of my life which is so full of rules. I live by a rigid schedule, up at dawn, a daily workout, always the first one to office and the last to leave. And then there is my job – which involves regulating financial discrepancies, so all I did all day was enforce other people's rules. But it wasn't always this way. I think back to a time in my life when I, like these children, was absolutely free.

Following my tenth-standard exams, I went back to my grandmother's for the summer break like I did every year. Here each day passed by painfully slowly, one long dosa-filled lunch stretching out into a chai-filled evening as I was dragged from one distant relative to the next. These relatives always spoke to me about how brave and handsome my father had been, and how beautiful and fashionable my mother, and told me anecdotes about my parents which I had heard so many times before.

'Your father was such a strong man, who served the country in many dangerous zones.' It seemed to me like my father would have been a perfect fit for Residency School, much more than I. My mother, they said, looked just like an actress and that she was the apple of my father's eye. I couldn't imagine how I, of all people, could be the son of such a lady.

Earlier, these relatives had seemed kind and sweet, and their stories interesting, but now they just seemed boring and their stories, repetitive.

I also began noticing how different I was from any of them. I dressed differently than my cousins or young boys, always tucking in my shirts, never leaving my house without a collared shirt or with dirty shoes; I ate differently too, never using my fingers even with rotis and rice, because it was not allowed at our school. The most noticeable thing though was the way I spoke. My English and even Hindi was distinctly different from everyone around me. All of my cousins spoke in what the junior school matrons called pigeon English, rapping us on the knuckles if we even used one word. As for my grandmother, she began sounding more and more like the administrative staff at school.

There were other discoveries too. I had always thought all schools were like Residency School, but I began realizing that the school I went to wasn't a normal sort of school. I remember my grandmother telling a distant aunt that I was a student of Residency School; she dropped her samosa and her eyes became as round as a tea cup. I began noticing more and more how people treated me differently when they found out that I went to Residency School and that too on a scholarship – my grandmother always mentioned this fact – and also my stellar marks, as if she were the one responsible for all of it. They asked me annoying questions. Residency School had featured in a few films and they asked me, star-struck, if that was how the school really looked. They made me speak to their children, who usually did not have an iota of interest and then they always made me promise to tutor them to pass the entrance exam of the school. I usually took one look at these dull-eyed children, thought of my muscle-head tutees and immediately missed Residency School, even the nerve-wracking times of the board exams.

Looking back, I realize I was coming to understand for the first time that not only was I different, but that in some way I was privileged, which was the strangest thing for me to digest because I had never felt like this, not once in my life. This truth became further more evident when I noticed the other schools in town, the untidy uniforms, the dried-up lawns, and the buildings, smaller than our smallest junior school boarding house.

Why were we different? It wasn't that the children who came to Residency School were that rich, many were sons and daughters of erstwhile maharajahs who had lost much of their fortune over the years, and were studying on subsidized fees. But where they came from, they were important, and they brought that importance to the school. It wasn't anything blatant; we all wore the same shoes, socks and even underwear, but it was the way they walked, the way they wielded their bats, the way they flipped their hair. It was privilege from beginning to end, and this is the culture I soaked up like a sponge without even realizing it. It was also this privilege that now made me realize how banal everyone I came across in my grandmother's town was.

As the days went by in this small dreary place, with nothing to look forward to at all, I realized what an integral part of me Riya had become. She was the first thing that I thought of when I woke up, the last thing that I thought of when I fell asleep, she was always there somewhere in my thoughts and now being away from her, it caused me almost physical pain. It was the strangest thing I had experienced. Thinking about the fact that I had 73 days, 1,752 hours and 105,120 minutes before I could see her again, my heart would swell and tremble and lurch, leaving behind pain worse than anything in my leg. When this heartache of mine was especially bad, I tried to sit down to write a letter to her, but then when I held my pen, no words came to me and I couldn't think of anything to write to her that wouldn't be really dumb. Plus, I knew that she wouldn't want to read anything beyond two to three lines.

Thinking about her so much, Residency School became to me a fantasy land; a verdant world of sparkling jade fields and its ruby red track with Riya like a vision loping around; the grand marble building with its sculpted dome, even my odiferous, noisy dorm seemed to be some sort of haven.

Earlier I felt that being here, being there, it was all the same, but for the first time I felt that Residency School was more my home than anywhere else and I wished very, very badly that I could be there.

After a while, I simply couldn't stand it any more and I feared that if I had to stay at my grandmother's for any longer, I would end up like my cousins – eating noisily, dressing untidily and watching pointless shows on TV. So I took the drastic step of writing fervent letters to the school saying that I had to come back to campus to study and prepare for engineering entrance exams. The authorities agreed to let me return – only because a student getting into IIT would be as good for them as it would for me – and twenty-one days after I had arrived, I departed from my grandmother's home and came back to my own. Yes: after ten years, Residency School had finally become my home.

24

WHEN I RETURNED to campus, it was as quiet as a stone. The pattering of small feet, the hoots of rowdy students, the shrill cries of bells and whistles, the organized chaos of our school, all gone, replaced now with a campus so silent that I could hear the warm whisper of the summer winds on the tracks and the rustle of the summer leaves on the deserted roads. The playing fields stretched green, empty and wide, the deserted buildings seemed to sigh in relief and the animals and birds of our school seemed to run uninhibited, as if they too were momentarily free of all the rules.

When I first arrived, used to a campus life full of rules, I felt confused and paralysed but I devised a tactic of thinking of my grandmother's stifling house and my relatives, after which I would immediately feel relief. So like this I quickly settled in.

It was to be one of the best summers of my life – just me, my books and her. Boarding school life had programmed me to operate on a schedule, to live by the bell, but for the first time since I could remember, time, which had always held me in thrall, did not matter at all. I woke up when I wanted to, no matron, no prefect, no grandmother jostling me out of bed. There were no bells going off, there were no classes to go to, no teachers to be afraid of, no prying eyes, no bullies to avoid.

I didn't have to report to PT at 6.00 a.m., I didn't have to wait in line for the bathroom, or warm up the pot for a senior, I didn't have to wait in dread for the sting of the bell. For the first time in my life, I didn't even have to make my bed.

I was meant to be studying for the IIT exams, but since there was no one supervising me, I spent most of my day time lying around under the deodar and chinar trees, taking in the scent of the wild roses and the buddleia, reading books from the library, gazing for hours at night at the stars that I loved, living in some sort of a glorious reverie, floating about, letting my hair grow out, not even bothering to put oil in it sometimes.

Riya trained with her coach in the morning, spent all afternoon sleeping, and then every evening, after dinner in the near-empty mess, I would meet her by the running track, and I would point out the stars to her in the indigo sky. There was the Great Bear lying on his back, and then the Swan, winging out of the Milky Way, then the Pegasus, like Riya, soaring above them all, and then my favourite, the gentle Shepard fading slowly with the dimming light of the moon.

The best part of the summer though was watching her run – this is when Riya was at her glorious best. Riya always said what was on her mind, never mincing words like other girls, but it was only through running that she really expressed herself. Through movement. Through the joy of kinetic energy. This was the essential truth of her: she was a body in motion; she could never be held or contained. Sometimes before a meet, on what was meant to be her day of rest, she would do some casual practice on the tracks. She invited me to these practices and I would be at the tracks at 4.00 p.m. sharp, stopwatch in hand, standing under the pavilion by the scoreboard, with a notebook to record her times. The heat was often oppressive, and I almost never had anyone to talk to, but I never got bored, no matter how many laps she took around that track. She ran slightly tilted forward, weight lowered, chin up, it almost looked like she was falling over, step by step, the ground catching her every time. She ran on her toes, and kept me on mine as well.

'Specs, you aren't paying attention,' she grumbled one afternoon, rubbing her hand across her sweaty face, leaving a trail of mud behind.

'I am,' I said, fumbling with the stopwatch that lay switched off in my palm. I had been distracted for a moment by a buzzard wheeling lazily in the azure sky.

'Every second matters, you know. The timing has to be exact,' she said crossly, placing her hands on her tiny waist, her face flustered and pink as she walked towards me catching her breath.

'I'm the one who's good with numbers, remember?' I joked.

'Those are your kind of numbers, Specs, and these are mine. Last time you stopped the stopwatch five seconds too late.'

'That wasn't me. It was you who was slow,' I said with a grin; nothing could get me in a bad mood these days.

She glowered and before I knew it she had taken off, kicking a cloud of dirt into my face.

And that is how I remember her, dancing and dazzling, disappearing into a dramatic sun.

And in this manner, one dreamlike day passed into the next.

25

I SAW A lot of B.P. that summer. It had its pluses and its minuses. Mostly it was a matter of convenience.

After a freezing winter, Residency School was experiencing its warmest summer in twenty years, the mountain sun so strong that it sometimes burnt our skins. Riya often insisted that we go over to her house rather than sit smouldering underneath the drying trees. I squeaked my protests and tried to stay away, preferring to keep my distance from all sports-related people, and B.P was the *head* of all sports and I was awfully scared of him; but I always relented, because we had no other place to go and it wasn't possible for me to deny Riya anything.

Her house was located on the far end of campus, bordering the dense coniferous forests that stretched out for hundreds of miles, where sometimes boys would venture out on a trek. From her garden, you could see the dome of the main school building and the spire of the chapel. If I strained my eyes I could see the roof of the red brick Ashok House, which was a fifteen-minute walk away.

The bungalow itself was old and spacious with high ceilings, scarred wooden floors and peeling white walls. The drawing room was sparsely furnished with only a few old chairs and a khaki sofa – nothing like the upholstered, colourful mess of my grandmother's home. In this bare room in a glass case were enclosed at least two dozen glittering trophies, B.P.'s large ones and Riya's small ones.

Riya's bedroom, like the rest of the house, was bare, almost like a dorm room, except that it was very untidy, strewn with pieces of clothing, hair ties and notebooks. If I had made a mess like this, Ansari Sir would surely have beat me with his cane. The most eye-catching thing in the room was a large blue plastic globe, sitting brightly in the middle of a small wooden desk. I wondered what it was doing there. It was only later that I found out about Riya's keen interest in the world.

B.P. was different from what I had expected, not the angry cricket coach who blew his shrieking whistle, or the strict man whose orders not even Vikram could disobey. I discovered that at home he had a surprisingly gentle demeanour, and I would often find him sitting in a chair, wearing cricket whites, reading Rumi or Ghalib.

In this house also lived Jeevan Singh, a wrinkled manservant who had been with B.P. even before Riya was born. He was the cook, the housekeeper and also Riya's nanny, ironing her uniforms, mending her socks, plaiting her hair and cutting it when it got too long.

Jeevan Singh was enormously and indeterminately old, somewhere between seventy and ninety. He was like an oak tree, a being whose existence defied time and epoch: it didn't matter when he began; it only mattered that he was, only ever wearing B.P.'s discarded cricket whites, or in this case yellows, which hung loosely around his hunched, shrivelled frame.

While B.P. didn't seem to mind my presence in the house – I felt that most of the time he didn't even notice when I came and went – Jeevan Singh seemed to detest me, giving me ice-cold stares and making vicious comments under his breath, never even offering me a glass of water or cold coffee, though he supplied Riya with both of these. During our meetings, Riya and I usually sat on the verandah under the fan; but even here Jeevan Singh would totter out and make such unfriendly faces that I often thought it best to leave. Riya noticed it, of course. It was impossible to miss Jeevan Singh's dislike. But she just shrugged it off.

'Ignore him,' she advised. 'He's just old.'

I followed Riya's advice as far as I could. I tried being more respectful, leaping to my feet whenever he entered the room, smiling widely at him, and carrying trays of used utensils back to the kitchen to save him the trouble. Nothing worked, in fact it just made it worse, and Jeevan Singh started playing pranks on me, hiding my shoes, spilling a cup of hot water on me 'by mistake', telling me that Riya wasn't around even when I could clearly hear her voice. Once, he even locked me in the bathroom where I remained for thirty minutes, too meek to create a fuss, politely knocking until Riya let me out.

Jeevan Singh, I realized, was a bigger bully than most boys at my school, but if his jibes were the price to pay for her friendship, Vikram had trained me well, and I was well prepared.

Plus, I hoped that when school started in a few weeks, I would have to see a lot less of the ancient grouch.

26

A SINGLE THOUGHT burdened us, gaining weight as the summer days passed us by. The day of our board exam results was approaching. Mostly, I tried my best to ignore it. Mostly, this didn't work. These exam results were all-important. My tenth-grade board results would determine if I was eligible for the scholarship which would allow me to stay at Residency School. I was confident that I had done well, but I knew that any number of slip-ups were possible – the examiner could mark a correct answer incorrect, copies could go amiss, marks could be miscalculated.

But I was more nervous about her than I was about myself. She had said she had done 'okay'. This could mean anything. She treated exams like one of her races, not looking back once she crossed the finish line. But as D-day approached, she grew very nervous. I could tell by the way she chewed her nails, by her increased fidgeting. Most of all, I could tell because her timings were totally off.

Seeing Riya like this – always so cool and confident – filled me with doubt. She had alluded to failing once or twice, but I had not taken her seriously. Until now. If she failed, the consequences would be dire. She would be held back, she would not be allowed to run, and she would not be able to go to another school in the area, because there was no other school within several hundred miles of where we were.

I realized with a lurch that if she failed, she would have to move to another town and repeat tenth grade. I knew there was nothing as embarrassing as having your classmates move up while you stayed in the same grade. I had seen it happen with a few students at school, and I didn't want it to happen to her.

And what would happen to me if she went away? I thought once again of those dire days I had spent at my grandmother's without her and what they had done to me. No, life without Riya was unimaginable. She simply had to pass.

That year the Central Board of Secondary Education had put the board marks on the internet, so both of us went to the Residency School's computer lab to check our marks online.

I entered my roll number – which I still knew by heart – on the keyboard and the numbers appeared slowly, line by line, less due to suspense, more due to the age of the computer and the speed of the internet. I looked down at my feet and closed my eyes and held my breath for so long that I began feeling dizzy.

She tapped me on the shoulder.

'Specs?'

Her face said it all, her glowing eyes, her ecstatic smile. I immediately felt relief. Then I saw the screen– a row of high 90s, even one 100 per cent. High marks, difficult for anyone to beat. Even Mrinalini.

She stared at the screen wordlessly, her eyes very still, I like to think it was awe; or maybe she was just very nervous because her marks were up next.

The computer lab was quiet except for the occasional hiss and hum of the machines and we were the only two people here. She fumbled around for the scrap of paper with her roll number and then dictated it to me as I punched the numbers in. As we waited, the internet now excruciatingly slow, she held my hand for the first time in my life.

So many things it seemed were happening all at once. Her hands, like her handwriting, were rough and hard like a boy's, her fingernails short and sharp, bitten at several places with bits of cuticles flying about. Mine, I thought embarrassed, were soft as cotton wool, a little too soft for a boy, even if he like me couldn't play sports.

In theory, holding hands should have been romantic, but she gripped my hand so tight that I thought something would break, then the server crashed, and we both let out a sigh of relief.

With a gulp and a deep breath, my palms now clammy as a frog, I re-clicked the mouse and now her marks popped up on screen.

Mathematics: 68 (68!)

English: 70

Social Science: 72

Science: 69

Hindi: 56

They were the highest marks she had ever scored in her life. She had never crossed a 50 in mathematics; here she was at a 68. She let go of my hand and stared at the screen, her eyes blinking very fast and her mouth a little 'o'. Neither of us said a word.

'I passed, Specs, I passed,' she finally whispered.

I really wished that at moments like this, she would call me Nikhil.

'You didn't just pass, you did well,' I said slowly, stunned by the results.

'Are you so surprised?' she said, turning sideways and looking at me with merry eyes.

'No! I … I…' I stuttered back.

That was Riya: at any time, in any circumstance, she knew how to get me in a bind.

And with that she threw her head back and she laughed, for almost a minute. She laughed until tears ran down her face.

Over the years I have developed a kaleidoscope of Riya, visions of that face that brought me so much joy. Riya laughing, the way she did with her mouth wide open, her little white teeth on display; Riya angry, when her eyebrows would curl into sharp little Vs; Riya sad, her face blank as a chalk board; Riya thinking, three creases in her forehead. Riya on the brink of victory, her nose scrunched up into a tiny ball. But this one moment, this moment, of Riya laughing, happily, freely, joyfully; this memory has been so much a part of me over the years that though I might try to forget everything about her, I know I will never forget this. It is my after-image of Riya, the way you see bright spots after the flash of a camera. And I still hear it ringing, dancing, always free.

27

ALL THINGS COME to an end, the good ones with surprising, manipulative haste. Our summer had reached its last act, the first chill of the northern breeze already in the air. The glorious blooms of summer – the scarlet rhododendrons and the sapphire delphiniums – were starting to fade.

Though I had not attended any classes, it was the most instructive summer of my life because for the first time, I felt like I learned what it means to live.

I learnt how to laugh openly, how to feel freely, and how to break the rules. And I had Riya to thank for all of that. Around her I did not feel like a shadow, a ghost; she challenged me to assert myself, to say what I really felt. Because of her, I was beginning to feel like a person I never thought I could be – someone confident and funny and strong, someone who had the courage to act for himself.

But, before the summer finally ended once and for all, there was one more thing that had yet to be learnt.

'Try it, Specs,' she pleaded with me, brandishing an old bicycle, lovingly polished, nothing like the multi-gear monstrosity that Vikram sometimes rode around school. 'You'll love it. I swear.'

Our campus was over a hundred acres from the tip of the south cricket field to the beginning of Dhobi Ghat. Many students rode bicycles. I, with my bad leg, had never considered cycling because it had always seemed like an impossible act. She was asking so nicely but I did not want to look like a fool: I pictured myself toppling face-first off that old bicycle and landing hard on the tarmac.

'I can't Riya,' I said more harshly than I meant to.

'Specs,' she pressed. 'I know you're worried. But it's not as hard as it looks. I spoke to Papa about it too.'

I was startled. 'Spoke about what?'

'About you riding a bike. Papa said that you could do it, you can use mostly your right leg, and once you gain momentum…'

Riya trailed off when she saw the look on my face. 'You spoke about me to B.P.?'

I stared at her for a second, infuriated. My weakness had been a topic of conversation? How could she do that when he probably already thought I was a wimp?

I don't know what madness came over me, but with my good leg I kicked the bike hard. My good leg was stronger than people thought and the bike flew through the air, and landed close to Riya, who gingerly stepped away. For a second she was angry, and was about to say something rude to me but she shut up when she saw my face.

Her face had fallen, her smile had dimmed and she said to me, 'I'm sorry, it's just that I thought it would be fun.'

She called out to Jeevan Singh to take the bike away.

I saw her looking with disappointment at the bike and then just as I reached the crest of my rage, I suddenly calmed down. I bent down and picked up the bike from the ground, its spokes still swirling wildly around. Holding my breath, and with quite some effort, I swung my good leg over the seat, settled my weight and used my arms to haul my bad leg to the pedal. Then I pushed off, wobbly, shaking to and fro, but still very much on the bike. I picked up speed and watched as the asphalt became a blur. Triumphant, I made the mistake of turning around to find Riya; and, just for a few seconds, before I came tumbling off, exactly as I imagined I would, I knew what it felt like to fly.

So this is how she feels, I remember thinking, as I soared delicately into a flowering shrub.

28

THE ELEVENTH STANDARD was a chance for a new beginning, and I was determined to take it.

For most of my life at Residency School, I had been left to my devices. Teachers liked me but did not love me (unlike Mrinalini); most students tolerated me but did not hate me. I had my place in this ecosystem, carved geologically, over a vast expanse of time. I'd never had the courage to disrupt the system – nor, truthfully, the inclination. So I accepted it as it was. That is, till Riya came along.

With her in my life, I knew that I would not be happy any more being that obscure, skinny guy with his head stuck in his books, his spectacles slipping off his nose. I did not want to be that spineless fool that people like Vikram could jerk around. I still hated myself for how I had backstabbed Riya because I was scared of simply being hurt.

I did not know how I would change, or whether I could. All I knew was that I could not be the same person that I had been for all of these years.

I decided to look at my situation step by step, rather than all at once – like I did with difficult sums.

For starters, I could no longer be an eleventh-standard walker and runner. Since sports were compulsory in our school, people like me were shunted into 'walk and run', which, in essence, was simply an hour of walking and running up and down an empty road. My walk-and-run status was pathetic, especially with B.P. being such a great sportsman and with Riya being the running prodigy that she was. So I called in a favour.

An enterprising tenth-standard student had recently started a chess team. He owed me: the previous year, I had lent him my ninth-standard science notes, after his had been stolen. This kid was slightly savvier than most of the academically inclined students, and far better connected since his father was a local magnate of some kind. There was a deal in place – his father sponsored the chess team, while he got to choose his squad.

It was a version of the King's Indian Attack, a chess tactic that I had read all about, meant to be used *only* in cases of overwhelmingly poor odds. I wheeled and cajoled and even sort of threatened the kid, and in the end I became the sixth boy on the Residency School chess team: my first-ever sport. And that was the end of my walk-and-run days. Here on the chess team, I found myself perfectly and entirely capable, and after I had beaten everyone hollow they were forced to make me captain of the team.

Academically, I had opted for the science stream – this was expected, since I was the topper of the school – and here I found my fit because paying attention in class didn't make you the butt of all jokes and high marks earned you respect rather than mockery. While I missed some of the 'lighter' subjects like history and literature, I finally had the chance to immerse myself deeply into the subjects I loved – physics, chemistry and my beloved mathematics.

Being a science student meant being separated from Riya, who had taken humanities. Though I missed her desperately – stealing glimpses of her during class had become so vital to my day – I knew that taking humanities would enable her to spend more time doing what she liked most, which was to run. Riya had no interest in sums or science, or history, or any subject at all. Riya was guided by her DNA, by God, or whoever decided our purpose on this planet for only one thing. She may have been a snail, a turtle, a donkey when it came to class but on the track, she was a winning racehorse who was a wonder to watch.

As for dorm life, my streak of luck continued. Ansari Sir decided to move the science students out of the dorms and into rooms, so they could focus on their studies. I found myself sharing a room with another science student who was almost as uninterested in sports as I was, and spent most of his time doing Sudoku and quietly preparing for the IITs.

I loved my tiny room, no matter how cramped it was. It provided a perfect hideaway from dorm life, with its noisome amenities and uncertain comraderies. Most importantly, it provided me a break from Vikram, something I needed now more than ever before. Now that Vikram had no use for me – he, like Riya, had taken humanities – whatever little semblance of friendship that we earlier had, vanished. He began taunting me like in mean little ways – grabbing the glasses off my nose and flinging them on the ground, or snatching a book out of my hands and throwing it into the dustbin. During morning assembly, he would pass embarrassing public remarks on the patches on my pants, the cheap quality of my shoes (the local brand that mostly the junior school kids wore), the oil in my hair (I had cut back on it, but it was a childhood habit, and I could not rid myself of it). An onlooker may have thought of all this as tomfoolery, but Vikram had mastered the craft of bullying over many long years and his antics felt like pointed, well-thought-out stabs at all my weak spots.

This was the only blemish in an otherwise flawless term. But, even Vikram couldn't bully me as much as he may have liked, because I still had my old students on my side. Each of the athletes I had taught the previous term ended up passing with better marks than they had ever gotten in any subject at any time in their lives, and while I had expected that they would forget all about me in the eleventh standard, it turned out their goodwill had not yet run out.

One night, as I sat at my little desk in my room, ensnared in double and triple bonds, I was jolted by a rap so loud the door almost flew from its hinges.

'Nikhil,' said a gruff voice in a gentle tone.

'Yes?' I asked alarmed, pushing my glasses up my nose.

'It's me,' the voice said, and a muscle head, his big frame contained in tiny shorts, suddenly materialized in my small room.

'He-llo-o,' I said quietly, a feeling of dread overtaking me, wondering why he was here and what he wanted from me.

He nodded vigorously for no reason at all, maybe it was some sort of reflex action that took place when he looked at me. I remembered all the times I had looked at him after explaining a sum and asked, 'Understood?'

'We got you something,' he said, pushing a little package into my hand so hard that I almost fell.

'Huh?' I said, hoping that this was not a prank.

The muscle head had a vague look of gratitude in his eyes. 'It's from all of us. For helping us,' he said, fumbling around, in an embarrassed tone.

'Oh,' I said, a little confused. 'Thanks.'

My guest then left, bumping his large frame into the bunk bed on the way out.

I opened the red, shiny wrapping on the small box. Inside was an expensive Walkman, peacock blue and silver. I could tell it was imported, from the glossiness of the box and the many labels that were stuck to it.

I had never received such an expensive gift. My grandparents used to send cash for my birthday, but that had stopped a few years ago, because they probably just forgot the date.

I sat there for a few moments, holding the Walkman, taking in the weight and the scent, plastic and perfume, the smell I would associate with all things precious for years to come. Only one thought occurred to me – how great would it be for Riya to run with music.

29

I AM DRIVING now and everywhere there are blue-green mountains and little clouds that rise like puffs of smoke in the sky. In them I see her here, then there and then also over there. I realize now that she, her memories, are like these mountains – too strong, too high, too difficult for me ever to scale.

A few years ago, I had tried to scale a mountain as part of a team-building exercise. Just like that mountain, Riya had brought me so much pleasure, but she had also brought me pain. In the early days of that journey, my leg was in constant pain, till slowly my body became used to it and the pain became part of my being. And then in one sudden moment I discovered pleasure in the pain. With Riya too, the worst pain had been in the beginning and not at the end.

The annual function was an important event in the Residency School calendar. Teachers rushed around preparing for the one day of the year on which the entire Board of Governors would descend. The gardeners, the sweepers, the maids and peons scrubbed every bit of the campus, till even the leaves on the trees seemed to shine. As for the students, the motivated ones spent weeks preparing skits, plays, dances and musical performances; the unmotivated ones took this opportunity to bunk endless classes, saying that they had to 'practise', but instead going off to take naps in the dorm.

On the night of the annual function everything seemed transformed under a magical spell. The buildings worn with age sparkled as if they were new, the impromptu stage felt like a dais, a grandstand, when just till the day before it had been a bunch of dusty poles and creaky boards. Our school band, usually horrendously out of tune during the morning assemblies when they played all sort of religious songs, managed to get their act together and put together an uplifting show. Even our formal uniform, grey trousers, white shirt, blazer and tie – the same we wore every Saturday – somehow looked different, much smarter and even the people who wore them seemed transformed.

I always wondered if I too was under this spell; if I too exuded magic like the rest of them. But when I looked into the hazy mirror, I generally found that I looked very much the same – skinny, with my faded long pants that hung more loosely around my left leg, black hair oiled and parted at the centre and the spectacles which took over most of my face.

The annual function truly was like no other night on campus. There was a sense of carnival, and everyone seemed to dance to its heady tune. This was the only evening of the year when there was no prep, no attendance, no teachers watching and even special food. Students ran amok, laughing and shrieking, up to all sorts of mischief until the small hours of the morning, and for once, no one bothered to check. The teachers, wanting to make an impression on the board and all the important guests, seemed for once to forget about the students. The prefects too were so busy collecting prizes that they forgot all about discipline. And so on the night of the annual function, it felt like none of the rules applied. In mathematical terms, it was a function without any limits at all.

Perhaps the most exciting part of the annual function were the seniors who had graduated the previous year and who returned on this day to claim their awards. The boys swaggered like grown-up men, dashing and debonair in their suits. The girls floated about like graceful sari-clad swans – so different than the awkward uniform-clad geese of just a few months ago.

Ordinarily, I would have used this time to read in peace, but that evening, even I had gotten caught up in the excitement. Obviously, this year was different – because of her.

The evening began with students performing skits, dances and plays that they had prepared for months. Although Residency School did not particularly prioritize the dramatic arts, many of these performances were very good. They had to be: Principal Sir let it be known that if we embarrassed the school in front of the visitors, we would be in deep trouble. After the plays came the lectures, first by Principal Sir, then the chief guest – a politician – who spoke so lengthily, and so incomprehensibly, that the audience was almost stupefied by the end.

Thankfully, the academic prizes were always the first to be given, probably because they were the least exciting for everyone. Every year without fail, I had been a part of the award ceremony, because for the past eleven years, I had been ranked first in my batch. Still, I got increasingly anxious as my turn approached. This stage seemed very large and high and to climb it wouldn't be easy for me, especially because I had been standing for such a long time and my leg was going numb. Riya stood a little behind me amongst the sportspeople, who were rowdy and loud; a stark contrast to the academics, who stood silent and orderly in a straight line.

I tried not to turn around and stare at her, but right before I had to go on stage, I could no longer resist. There she stood scratching the back of her right leg with her left shoe, her hair tied tightly in a mandatory braid, her face flushed under the bright lights of the canopy, her eyes bright with the excitement of the night. Transfixed, I would have kept staring, but then a boy elbowed me and I saw that it was my turn to go up on stage. It went off as smoothly as it possibly could. I hobbled up on stage, a line of students trailing me, and shook the hand of the chief guest as the photographer blinded us with his flash. Ansari Sir handed each student their 'prize' – a book no one read but which was used to prop up their tables, chairs and beds. It was all over in a few seconds, and we were herded into a waiting area close to the stage.

I looked at the stage, where things had become heated as the athletes swaggered across the dais in their particular way – chests out, legs bowed, arms a few inches away from their body, reminding me of the apes I had seen on TV.

The real commotion began as the athletic cups were distributed – the epitome of success at our school that each house vied for all year long. The clapping – which for us academics had been tepid and lethargic – had now become loud, accompanied by howling, whistling and thundering shout-outs. I saw Riya go up to get her prize, walking straight, chin up in the air, her skirt swinging like a pendulum. I clapped until my hands were sore. And then, there came Vikram, who even I had to admit, looked formidable in his blazer and tie.

My attention waned once Riya had received her award. I couldn't talk to her: she was still amongst the sports people, cheering and hooting for the seemingly unending procession of sports acknowledgements that became almost comical in their permutations and combinations – best bowler, best fast bowler, best spin bowler. As I watched, one thing began plaguing my mind. I had to pee so badly that I could hardly stand. I slipped away from the waiting area and walked as fast as I could to the bathroom, sorely resisting the urge to relieve myself in the fields.

Feeling much more relaxed after the visit to the bathroom, I dallied in the quadrangle and then decided to head back to the dorm and read. I had been hoping to catch Riya, to maybe talk to her, but on a night like tonight, with so many people around, I knew that we would probably not get a chance.

I walked back, whistling a tune that some junior school kids had danced to tonight, and crossed the dark academic block, so quiet and serious now compared to the rowdy stage. Just as I was contemplating taking a shortcut through one of the classrooms, I heard the tremor of a voice I knew so well, a voice that I could recognize from miles away, a voice that often came to me in my dreams.

How could this be? Here at this time?

I stood there and everything was so quiet that I could hear the breeze blowing through the trees. Then I heard it again, and then I saw the light shining from a single classroom.

Before I could fully understand what was happening, I found myself standing outside the classroom, looking through the grills of the window, staring at her standing with him next to the blackboard. The same classroom where I had tutored her, the same board on which we had solved hundreds of sums.

It couldn't be. It couldn't possibly be.

But it was.

There she was, *my girl* in flesh and blood, standing next to him. Abdul Sami Khan, the big man on campus last year, the former hockey captain of our school. I knew him – who didn't? He had walked around campus as if he owned the school despite continually getting into trouble with the teachers, who had to inevitably let him off the hook since he won so many accolades. I remembered him so clearly, short but broad, golden studs in his ears and long greasy hair that he slicked back. He was always surrounded by his band of boys, everyone looked up to him, even boys like Vikram. Now he was back in a fancy suit and tie, looking so much older than last year.

What was Riya doing here with him? And then, my head spun as I remembered snippets of things I had heard. Abdul had asked boys to deliver notes to her. He had once told a boy to fill her desk with rose petals and on another occasion had Vikram deliver chocolates on his behalf. But these were just the antics of boys and Abdul being Abdul could do as he pleased. Riya had always seemed so far removed from anything to do with this school that I never for a moment thought that she might have been involved with him. But maybe she and Abdul had been friends? If that had happened, how would I have known? But how could I *not* have known? I'd spent all those hours tutoring her, and then there were those long summer days, but then again we never spoke about such things.

My thoughts were broken with a sound. I saw him walking towards her, holding a small bottle in his hands. He took a swig, wiped his mouth with the back of his hand and then with a devilish grin, he handed the bottle to her.

No, Riya, no. Don't do this.

I wanted to scream, to stop her, but how could I? None of this was making any sense to me. She did not take the bottle from him but stared at him coolly and then he lurched towards her and put the bottle to her lips. She did not resist but swallowed slowly and then she moved away.

She did not speak much. Neither did he. She just looked at him obscurely, her smile small and fixed.

Then he stepped forward, towards her, and she, she did not move. He reached over to her and then bent his head down towards hers. No. No. No. Those lips, those were mine. I clutched the grill with all my might and then I dropped the book I was holding and it landed on my foot and tumbled to the ground.

They both looked up towards the window, startled, like wild animals caught in a hunt. I moved away as quickly as I possibly could, but it was me, and I simply wasn't fast enough.

30

EVEN NOW, AFTER everything that happened, those days strike me as the most painful, as if someone had punched me very hard, making my blood rush to my head, my head spinning round and round. It's the one time that I never want to think about, but it's the one that haunts me to this day. I had made the discovery of not being loved and there was nothing worse in this world.

Following the annual function, I avoided her completely. I did not meet her in the academic block during tea, I did not meet her at the art block after games, I did not even go watch her practise on the tracks. I fell into a dark dark place, into a void growing deeper and wider every day. I had always prided myself on having an orderly mind, on always acting sanely, on always being in control. All that fell away, like so many of my other dreams, and I, too, gradually began to fall apart.

I did everything, attended classes and assembly, even did my homework, but I went through it all getting sucked deep into the mud.

Everything felt like it took a vast amount of effort but even though I was so tired I could not sleep. Every time I closed my eyes, I wondered about her. How could she do this to me? What had she done? Was everything I had with her a total lie?

I had so many sleepless nights that I contracted a fever and was sent to the infirmary. Even then, sleep eluded me. My bones felt like they were breaking, my joints felt like they were snapping, I ached in places I hadn't known could ache. I writhed and turned and tossed. Often, I was sure that I could never get up ever again.

Some part of my brain told me – still tells me – that I didn't have a right to be angry. Riya wasn't mine. She may have liked boys before. She may even have kissed them. But the thought of Riya with anyone else, made me feel small and helpless and miserable so I just held my head in my hands, too sick and tired to shed another tear.

How strange loss is, how permanent and implacable. I was an orphan, I didn't really have a home. Of all people in the world, I thought I knew the real meaning of loss. Now I knew how very arrogant I had been.

Days went by and I stayed in the infirmary till finally the fever dropped and I began sleeping in fitful bursts. I was sent back to my room, where my fretful roommate tended to me diligently: I think he was frightened I would breakdown, go berserk, ruin his carefully written notebooks. I did no such thing. I was tired, weak and could do nothing but think about her. I simply shut down and went into hibernation, tapping into the ways of my childhood when I hardened myself till nothing could affect me any more.

Then, one afternoon, as I walked slowly, zombie-like, to chess practice – it felt like it took superhuman strength to simply get through the motions of the day – I heard a familiar gait behind me and suddenly I felt I would faint.

'Specs,' she called. 'Wait.'

She was almost behind me, but I didn't say a thing and continued on my way.

She sped up till she was right by my side. Even now, even after everything, having her right next to me, did something crazy to me.

'I tried to come see you so many times,' she explained, laughing. 'But those nurses … they are worse than Ansari Sir.'

I stopped now, but didn't say a word, little things going off in my brain.

We stood there for a while till at last she announced in a small trembling voice, 'I'm sorry.'

'For what?'

'You know for what.'

What could I possibly say?

'Specs, I didn't meant to … I…' she trailed off.

I stared fiercely at the rubble by her feet, cutting her off abruptly. 'But you did.'

I had a sudden image of her, of them, looking at the window, his gaze furious, hers very pained.

We were silent for a moment. I took a breath, trying to quell the sudden buzzing in my ears.

'It was a mistake,' she said slowly. 'I don't know what got into me.'

I didn't say a word, but a hard knot of air was forming in my chest.

'Specs…'

I locked my eyes with hers. She nodded and turned her face away.

'But how could you do that with him?'

She took a deep breath.

'I don't know, Specs … everything just got to my head.'

The questions were bitter, ripped from me, a torrent I had been swimming in day and night.

'Why did you go with him? Why did you drink that? Why did you, Riya?'

I went on like a broken record, asking the questions which had been whirring in my head night and day.

She said nothing for a moment and then finally spoke. 'I don't know, Specs. You know I can be stupid sometimes.'

I didn't open my mouth but I kept repeating the questions in my head over and over again.

She kicked the ground. 'I wasn't sure how you felt.'

'How I felt?' I said. I was now so angry at her that I spat out my words, 'Isn't it *obvious* that I've fallen in love with you?'

She looked at me strangely and now something flickered across her face.

'Specs…'

I looked away, burning, so embarrassed that I had finally said the words.

'You're being silly.'

Suddenly, something inside of me dropped away, very, very low. She was going to tell me that she didn't love me, that she didn't feel the same way.

But then she swung her hair out of her face, stepped towards me and whispered in my ear. 'You don't *fall* in love, Specs, you only rise.'

And then she came closer, my body touched hers, and her fingers touched mine and then she put her arms around my neck and for that single moment I felt totally complete.

And that is how we started, Riya and me.

31

IN THOSE DAYS, it wasn't common for boys and girls at Residency School to spend time together, and it was particularly strange for a boy like me. Co-ed friendships were the sole territory of the twelfth standard. Vikram, renowned ladies' man, was a notable eleventh-standard exception. I was not a renowned ladies' man. If my relationship with Riya came to be known, I would just be teased relentlessly, and even worse, Riya would be too.

So we kept it under wraps and we met secretly in places where there would be few students around, like the tracks after games time, the art block, or sometimes at her house.

We didn't even have tutoring any more because we had different subjects, though if I could have had the opportunity, I would have gladly learnt her new subjects to teach them to her. In all fairness to Riya, she didn't particularly need me, or anyone else. Her board results had boosted her confidence in an unexpected way, and she had permanently improved her academic standing across the board. She wasn't topping the batch, but she was average and that was more than she had ever been before.

Her running, however, was anything but average. She seemed to be continually improving, shaving micro-seconds off her personal bests, discovering hidden efficiencies within each footfall. The better Riya got – the more races she ran and won – the more she was away for competitions, winning medals in different parts of the state. That autumn, she was gone a lot, days at a stretch, sometimes even a week. Occasionally, I would get a postcard with some messy, brief scrawl – 'Specs, I won! Coming home now' – never signed with her name, in case someone in my house decided to go through my mail.

These postcards came to mean a lot to me, and I looked forward to them enormously. I knew that these postcards were the extent of what I could expect from Riya by way of romance because Riya wasn't a romantic sort of a girl. I, unfortunately, realized that I was a romantic kind of guy and I did little things, sometimes more for myself than for her. I penned poems for her and sappy notes. Often, I was so embarrassed by these that I never even gave them to her. I bought her chocolates (these she seemed to like) and after her spectacular board results, I got her a little pink teddy bear, with black beaded eyes. It was not exactly cute in the classic way, but it was the only thing that I could find in the one gift store in our small town.

She looked at it curiously and then put it in her bag. I was pleased to see it in her bedroom, propped on her bed, on a future visit. But then on another I happened to see it under her bed, brown instead of pink, gathering dust.

And so like that eleventh grade passed by as quickly as my girl ran around the track. I was engulfed by my studies, with complex numbers, trigonometric functions, laws of motion and chemical bonding.

And then there was another sort of bonding. Riya and I spent every free minute we had together, laughing, talking, walking. We got to know each other better than I would have thought possible. And the most amazing thing was, the minute I was sure I knew everything about her, she would surprise me with something more. Like the time I discovered that she could read French, or another time when I saw a trophy in her name for being on the Indian basketball team, and then another when she ate ten samosas and could have gone for more, but we had run out of money. I wanted to plumb her depths and just when I thought I had hit rock bottom, I realized that she was infinite.

32

THAT SUMMER, I had yet again managed to finagle my way back to Residency School for another bout of 'studying' for my engineering exams. This time, I hadn't even bothered to go to my grandmother's house. Judging by her silence, she wasn't too perturbed.

It was a funny feeling, watching the dorms vacate, the peons and drivers loading bags and trunks into their cars. I remember eating an apple picked straight off the tree and feeling very peaceful as the school slowly drained of all noise and dirt and chaos.

Life had a rhythm that Riya and I composed. I'd wake early and meet her at her house for breakfast. Then she would go train, I would slip off and read. In June and July, advised by the librarian, I worked my way through the classics. In August, I gave way to guilty pleasures and read only P.G. Wodehouse and Agatha Christie.

It's funny how time eludes our memories, blurs them, swirls them in fog. I remember very little of that summer except a sense of deep contentment. One day though stands out in particular. As I lay stretched out underneath a deodar tree, listening to the gentle whisper of the grass, watching the saffron and red marigolds splash colour everywhere, she sat next to me twirling the blue globe she had fetched from her desk, 'Do you know the capital of Bhutan?' she asked.

'Thimpu,' I said with my eyes closed.

'How did you know that?' she asked curiously.

'Ninth-standard geography. Unit 3, Chapter 2.'

'Really?'

'Yup,' I said with a smile and heard her scramble to her feet.

'So many places to go and here we are, stuck on this stupid mountain.'

'I like this mountain,' I murmured, half asleep, the heat of the sun seeping into my skin.

Impossibly restless, she paced the ground.

'Specs, wake up,' she urged.

I cocked one eye open and then shut it again. She stood by me impatiently, tapping her foot, hands on her tiny waist.

'Fine,' she grumbled. 'I wanted to show you the magazine Papa got about the country's best colleges.'

I froze underneath the glorious sun. College. Here, on this mountain, college seemed so far away. 'College is a long way away,' I mumbled.

She raised her eyebrows. 'Not that long.'

College. The thought depressed me. Residency School wasn't a perfect place – I knew that better than anyone else. But I couldn't imagine being anywhere else. It was the only world I knew, the only world I had. And with Riya in this world, the thought of leaving seemed so terrible I could scarcely face it.

All I wanted to do was to stay. All she wanted to do was to leave. There was a lightness and excitement in her voice whenever she talked about places far away. She spoke continuously of the future; of Delhi, of Mumbai, of Bengaluru, sometimes of London and the United States, all big places, all so far away. She spoke of her dreams too, the nationals, the Asian Games, sometimes even the Olympics and all the races in between.

I had not been anywhere significant other than the school. I had not travelled much, except for the occasional school trip. I remember how she looked at me when I told her that I had never been to Delhi. When I asked her why she was surprised, she just wrinkled her nose and shrugged.

'You just seem to know so much about so many places and so many things. I guess I assumed you had been everywhere.'

And then, after a pause, she added sagely: 'It must be all those books that you read.'

The irony of all of this was that the world truly was my oyster. With my marks, I could go anywhere and do anything that I wanted to. The teachers were beginning to ask me about my plans for the future, about the engineering exams that I had come back two summers to study for but really had no intention of taking at all. They were all very curious, especially Ansari Sir. This was expected – anything I achieved, I'm sure he would take credit for.

Riya, seeing that she wasn't getting anywhere with me, plonked down with a sigh and lay down next to me.

And then there we were, next to each other, but also so far apart. And all I could say to her was, 'Let's think about today.'

33

THE YEAR OPENED with its typical rituals. Sports teams were named, sections were assigned, new students were ragged and so many more, only one of which mattered to me – the handing out of new books, crisp notebooks and items of stationery – the one ritual I treasured over everything else.

There was one tradition though which loomed above the rest. At the beginning of every school year, twelve of the 'best' twelfth-standard students – two from each of the six houses – were crowned prefects, the pinnacle of Residency School success.

All my life, I had always watched these demigods from afar. They seemed set apart, like figures from a Greek allegory, halos crowning their heads, gold badges pinned to their chests. Prefects wielded more power and influence than all students, sometimes even teachers, controlling the student body, taking charge of their house, even wearing different uniforms which set them apart from the herd. They had their own common room, their own studies, even their own set of school rules. It seemed strange to me that this year these venerated beings would be appointed from amongst my own batchmates, boys I had seen cry, burp and sneeze their way through adolescence, right by my side.

As the annual naming approached, the school went into its normal frenzy and speculations were rife about who would be made prefect and thus control our lives. Boys placed bets on their favoured candidates, factions were formed, allegiances were pledged and boys were beaten up – a usual consequence of most situations at our school. I, as usual, remained in the shadows, a bystander of events that I neither cared to understand nor particularly wanted to be a part of – until in the strangest turn of events, I found myself not just involved but also in the eye of the storm.

'Papa thinks you have a chance at being a prefect,' said Riya as casually as if she was talking about clouds in the sky.

I stumbled and dropped the book I was holding in my hands. It fell in a puddle and I cursed silently. The librarian had warned me about my mistreatment of books.

I thought about what she had said for a moment and then decided that there was absolutely no chance.

'Maybe if all the other twelfth graders die. Which may not be a bad thing at all.'

'I'm serious,' she said.

Me? A prefect? It seemed preposterous. I had never once held a leadership position of any sort in this school.

However, B.P.'s endorsement was no small thing – he was on the selection committee, after all. Still, it made little sense to me. If I were unimpressive to anyone, wouldn't it be B.P.? Wouldn't he, of all people, want the cricket captain, or the hockey captain, or any of these sporty types to be prefect instead of a crippled, studious boy?

'That's ridiculous,' I finally said. 'Anyone has a better chance than me.'

'Why?'

'Sports,' I slowly said. 'I don't play sports.'

Riya sniffed derisively. 'Papa says that sportsmen never make good prefects.'

'They're always prefects here.'

'Not always good ones.'

I had never questioned the quality of our prefects, but B.P. did have a point.

'He says they're selfish and too self-absorbed. Kinda like me,' she said with a characteristically honest shrug.

'You're not like that!' I exclaimed in protest. 'You're the most … the most…'

'The most what?' she said, looking at me, a shadow of a smile on her face.

'You're the most amazing person I know.' No more eloquent words coming to my mind.

'Oh Specs,' she said, rolling her eyes.

'I'm just an ordinary person. There's nothing, not in the least bit, special about me.'

Her face was turned slightly away from me and her hair, after practice, was all over the place. But underneath her smugness and her hair, I thought I may have seen her blush, but it may have just been me.

34

RIYA LAID IT all out for me. Every teacher liked me and I was the best student in the twelfth standard. The chess team I captained had won a few state awards. Viswanathan Anand had just won the World Chess Championship for the first time and suddenly, it was the golden age of chess. Even in a sports-crazy school like Residency School, our team was getting some respect.

The prefecture, it seemed, was closer than I had ever thought. Once I realized this important fact, what had at first seemed impossible now began coalescing in my mind. Looking back, I realize that this was the beginning of a new me. For the longest time, I'd been content to simply occupy space. I was okay being Specs, the clumps of cells that studied science and lived on the second floor of Ashok House. No longer, not any more. Now I wanted to make a difference, I wanted to matter. For the first time in my life I wanted a proper place in this school.

So I began to plan. My academics, obviously, were outstanding. My extracurricular activities were less so. Except for the occasional writing and poetry competition, I had participated in very little. I thought of the possibilities – debate, elocution and anything that involved public speaking was out. The thought of going up on stage and speaking in front of so many people made me want to throw up. It was mandatory for every student to go on stage and read the news at least once a year. Many students enjoyed this – boys like Vikram loved the sound of their voice. I, on the other hand, dreaded my turn all year long.

My only possible hope was the general knowledge quiz. I had a knack for GK, and it was also something that I could prepare for. There was a pragmatic aspect to this decision: I'd been studying for tests my whole life; it was, in a real way, the only thing I was good at. The only problem was that the few times I had been on a GK team, I had gotten so nervous when our turn came around to answer the questions, even if I knew the answer, I usually froze. This time, though, I knew it would be different, it *had* to be different – I had to do it not only for myself but for her.

The annual GK quiz was coming up and it was a big deal in our school, almost as important as some of the sports competitions. I found it vaguely ironic that the only time people studied diligently was when there was a prize to be won: but this was Residency School. The competition was held over three days in the main auditorium and every house had to enter two two-person teams; after a few elimination rounds, the six best teams would compete for the cup.

It wasn't hard for me to find a partner. When it came to academics, everyone had full faith in me and I found a boy from the commerce section – an above-average bugger with a passion for the tabla – who was happy to leave all the preparation to me. That was fine by me: I wanted time to spy on the competition. There were two sharp eleventh-standard science students in Rajender House who between them knew every World Cup cricket score for the past fifty years. Mrinalini had teamed up with an enormous girl who apparently read five newspapers every morning. The topper in humanities had chosen a tiny squeaky-voiced science prodigy in tenth standard, who I affectionately – privately – thought of as 'young Specs'. But otherwise, there wasn't much competition.

Funnily enough, since our house was lacking in academic heavyweight, Vikram was chosen to take part. His agenda was the same as mine – everyone with prefectural hopes was participating in everything that they could. While Vikram was a definite prefect, he was really in the race for head boy. I didn't understand why *everyone* looked up to him – our school had somewhat of a herd mentality and they needed a leader, whoever it was. I figured this was the same way that Hitler rose to lead the Nazis.

As the competition approached, preparation became intense, as it did for all competitions at Residency School. Tricks were not uncommon at this stage: reference books went missing, encyclopaedias were defaced, library cards were stolen, and teams were sabotaged. Most important of all were the *Manorama Yearbooks*, which had been gathering dust in the corner all year, and for which now there was a fifty-person waiting line. But there were small advantages of holding the record for most number of books checked out in the school year. Librarian Ma'am reserved all the books I needed which I quickly hid under my bed, in case Vikram or someone else tried to steal from me.

I prepared and prepared, thinking of Riya running lap after lap on the track, day after day, no matter how tired she was. I was literally trying to cram all of modern history (of the world) in my head in just a matter of days. Riya helped me loyally, and after her practice, we would sit on the steps on the pavilion and in the dimming light of dusk, she would quiz me.

'Who was the prime minister during the Emergency?' she asked, reading slowly in a sing-song voice, like the students in the fifth standard.

'Indira Gandhi,' I said without hesitation.

'Wrong, Specs! You're finally wrong,' she said with a grin.

I adjusted my glasses. 'Firstly, I'm right, and secondly, you shouldn't be *happy* if I got it wrong.'

She brought the book close to her face, and then with a sigh, squinted at the page. 'You may be right, this writing is just so small!'

'Maybe you need some specs?' I said with a grin.

She gave me a look and put the book down on the steps. 'One pair between us is really enough.' Then, after a pause, she added, 'I just don't want you to get overconfident.'

'I won't,' I said truthfully: overconfidence was never my problem.

'You have to push the hardest towards the end,' she said.

'What if pushing hard makes you fail?' I asked, knowing that the more pressure I put on myself, the more nervous I would get.

'In that case, you just have to have faith.'

'Faith … in what?'

She said it like it was obvious.

'In yourself, Specs.'

'I don't know about that,' I said quietly, doubt written all over my face. 'The only person I have faith in, really, is you.'

'Well, that won't help right now, Specs. I can't even spell half the words in this book.'

And with that she got up, kicked her legs up, warming up, and went flying down the track.

35

THE FINALS ROUND of the GK quiz was held on a Saturday afternoon, which meant the whole school had piled into the auditorium to watch and cheer.

The first two rounds had been a breeze. We had won easily, and I hadn't even been nervous because there was hardly any audience at all. But now, for the finals, it seemed to me that every student at Residency School was here in this hall. The space was muggy, claustrophobic, filled with body heat, stale cologne and raw suspense. I felt choked in my blazer and tie, afraid that everything that I had studied would evaporate into thin air. My partner was not much comfort; he spent most of the time discreetly hyperventilating into a plastic bag.

The only consolation was Riya, in the third row, who wore red ribbons in her hair: her special good-luck charm, which she normally kept reserved for the most important races.

By some miracle, Vikram too had made it to the final round. I supposed he had made a wise choice of partners – the commerce topper, a fat Bihari boy with a stammer – who now sat there with a lazy grin on his face, waving and winking to his friends in the audience.

The competition was divided into four sections: geography, history, science and sports. Each of the six teams would be asked questions on these topics and then be eliminated after each round based on the number of correct answers. The panel of judges included Rao Ma'am, Principal Sir, and B.P. The three of them conferred silently, checking their questions and answers. I tried to keep my sight on Riya but as the auditorium filled up, all I could see was a sea of heads and hair.

And then a beeper went off, and we began.

They asked us question after question, giving us four options for each question as we went through each of the categories.

'Which is the largest Buddhist monastery in India?'

'Marasmus is caused due to the deficiency of which nutrient?'

'Which ancient Indian sage authored the *Yoga Sutras*?'

'What is India's fastest train?'

I was much too nervous to answer these questions myself so I whispered the answer into my partner's ear and he gave the judges our response, never doubting me even once. I figured this gave me an air of Svengali-like wisdom and power. It also meant no one would hear my voice shake. In those moments when I became stuck, completely blanking out, I thought of Riya, how she had once run a race with a fractured leg. It gave me spirit and we battled on.

At the very end, there were only two teams left – mine and Vikram's. In the audience section that was reserved for teachers, Ansari Sir clapped and screeched like a demented buzzard: it no longer mattered who won, since both teams were from the same house. But to me it mattered so much more now than before.

In the front row, Vikram's followers were roaring and stamping, thrilled that he had reached so far and urging him to win. But people were also curious about me, this unknown entity who had suddenly found himself in the hot seat. As the judges regrouped for the ultimate round, the tension reached a fever pitch.

As a special twist, we were to choose the question category for each other.

'Sports,' said Vikram, looking straight at me, a sneer on his lips.

'Science,' I replied, in a steady voice.

To this point in the competition, I'd been nervous, but suddenly I found myself enjoying the thrill of Vikram and I pitted against each other on a stage. We'd been friends. He'd tormented me. He'd protected me. He'd abandoned me. He'd made me hurt Riya. He'd shown me how weak I could be. It was time now to return the favour. It occurred to me that perhaps this is why people played sports – for this deep gladiatorial thrill.

The MC of the competition – a pretentious eleventh-standard boy from the GK Club who insisted he be referred to as the 'quizmaster' – declared that Bajwa Sir, the head of science would ask Vikram's team the final question while B.P. would ask us. Suddenly I no longer felt so confident. I would finally make a fool of myself in front of the very man I wanted to please so very much.

Bajwa Sir was a hirsute sardar with a white beard that covered most of his face. 'Boys,' he boomed. 'Are we ready?'

The room became instantly silent and a sort of distant hum began ringing in my ears.

'Which of the following is a non-metal that remains liquid at room temperature?'

If they knew the answer outright, they would get full marks; otherwise, they would ask for options and get less marks. For the briefest moment, I saw Vikram's mask of confidence drop.

'Sir, can we have options?' asked Vikram, visibly distraught for the first time in the competition.

'Phosphorous. Bromine. Helium. Chlorine.'

Tenth-standard chemistry. Chapter 6. Unit 2. Vikram and his partner whispered frantically to each other, and I knew then that neither of them had a clue. But there was still a twenty-five per cent chance of a lucky guess.

'Phosphorus, sir,' answered Vikram's partner nervously, just as their time ran out.

Their faces fell as the beeper went off – their answer was incorrect.

'The right answer,' said Bajwa Sir, 'B-ro-mine.' His wide grin, visible even under his beard, revenge on the boys who had never paid attention in class.

And now, it was our turn.

Their fault wasn't necessarily our win. We had to get the next answer right, or else we would have to face off all over again. Now B.P. cleared his throat. As ever, he sounded totally in control.

'Ready, boys?'

I could just about nod my head, it felt leaden like my leg. A fine sweat had gathered at the back of my neck and my palms were so slippery that I could barely hold the mic. Even my partner emitted a squeak of fear.

'Which cricketer is known as the father of Indian cricket?'

The timer was ticking, seeming to go faster than before. My partner looked at me, befuddled, I shrugged: neither he nor I had a clue. And then a memory slipped into my mind, a cover of a book, a single name. What was the name of that book? I tried very hard to remember and just as my partner was going to ask for options, I sputtered into the mic, 'Ranjitsinhji.'

Time seemed to stand still as B.P. spoke into the mic, 'Your answer is correct.'

One hot summer afternoon as I waited for Riya in her living room, I had picked up a copy of a book lying on the table, and begun leafing through the pages. Then B.P. unexpectedly walked into the door.

Startled, I jumped off my seat nervously. 'Good afternoon, sir,' I stammered.

He looked at me bemusedly, and then, seeing the copy of the book in my hand, he asked, 'Do you know who that is?'

I looked at the faded cover with the face of a smiling man. 'Uh, no sir.'

'The father of Indian cricket.'

And then Riya had walked into the room.

For our victory, both my partner and I received 2,000 rupees as prize money, a fortune for a boy like me. I decided that I would treat Riya to a feast at the tuck shop – samosas, imported chocolates, her favourite Maggi noodles and anything else that she wanted. For the first time in my life, I felt rich.

Riya smiled at me and then said to me with her mouth full of chips, 'You did it, Specs.'

'We did it!' I exclaimed.

She rolled her eyes. 'I didn't know the answer to a single thing.'

And she handed me a newspaper cutting of a small fuzzy picture of my partner and I smiling like idiots. The competition had been sponsored by the local newspaper and our victory had been in print.

'Papa wanted you to have this.'

I had decided not to say anything about B.P.'s complicity in my victory to Riya. Only because I did not know whether B.P. had done it on purpose or if it was sheer chance. All I knew was that if B.P. had done this for me, I would be ever grateful to him. Standing on that stage and accepting the trophy from Principal Sir had been one of the triumphs of my life. Vikram, I remember, had behaved strangely, stomping off stage, refusing even to shake my hand – which had caused murmurs for being such a flagrant violation of the school's chummy ethos to be a good sport no matter what.

The crunching of the chips that she noisily munched stirred me out of my thoughts. I looked at her reading the newspaper clipping carefully, tracing the tiny words with her finger.

'You know,' I said casually, putting a chip in my mouth. 'I think your father's starting to like me.'

'Oh no,' she said warmly, reaching for the ketchup, 'he doesn't like anyone at all.'

36

FOLLOWING THE GK quiz, Vikram lost a lot of face. It transpired that he had bribed a peon to steal the GK quiz notes from the club secretary, accounting for his unexpectedly strong performance until the final round. So in the days that followed, he kept an unexpectedly low profile. This, of course, was fine by me. I was in fact somewhat gleeful at Vikram's fall from grace. Uncharacteristically, I even joined in the gossip-mongering and rumour-spreading, but when I tried talking to Riya about it – jokingly rubbing it in – she only shrugged. 'Maybe he felt insecure.' This should have sounded an alarm bell, instead I only remember fondly marvelling at her depth of spirit and magnanimity.

Most people would never have noticed; but I had been a keen observer of Riya for years and I could see patterns and discern trends. My grandmother often said it was a gift, but sometimes it felt like a curse.

It was the little things at first. He would smile at her, actually *smile* at her, almost nicely; she would return the gesture with a smile that was familiar because it was reserved for me. Though I only ever saw them talking from afar, I could see from her body language that the iciness that had existed between them for the past two years seemed to have thawed.

For so many years, I had dreamt of being in a classroom on

the third floor of the science block, a serious science classroom, with other serious science students, no smart mouths like Vikram passing wisecracks from the back, but now I wished desperately that I was back in that tenth-standard classroom, dodging spit-balls and avoiding bullies, my eyes solidly fixed on Riya's back.

As I sat in the front of the class, dealing with a boggling derivative which I usually loved, I began obsessing, wondering what they were up to together in class. When Dominic Sir opened the window I heard the sounds of their laughter fluttering in, over the hasty scratching of our pens and sour smells of chemistry. I always imagined I could pick out the thread of her laughter, always sweet and surprisingly low-pitched. Now I began to think I could hear his as well.

Once, as I crossed the humanities department on my cycle, running an errand for a teacher, I saw Riya and Vikram talking in the hallway, and even from the distance I could see that he was attentive, and that she, with her books held close to her chest, had a smile on her lips.

Out of the classroom, things got worse. While discussing strategies with my chess team at Scindia Pavilion, I saw them on the track. Vikram was resplendent with his gelled hair, sculpted body and cocky grin, chatting with Riya, who wore shorts so long that they looked like a skirt. I saw him whisper something into her ear; she threw her head back, laughing, flipping the hair off her face. Then they both took off, him trailing as she led.

I stood there for a while, at a little distance from the tracks, watching her run, uselessly seeking her gaze, a great sorrow filling my heart. Most boys would get angry, their testosterone surging, and probably want to punch the other guy. Not me though, I just felt like crying, my heart coming up to my throat.

Swallowing my tears, I tried to rationalize it to myself. They were in the same class; they were both athletes, sometimes travelling together to various meets. It was natural that they would eventually become friends. But then I remembered the way he had teased her during her first few months at school, the blank look on her face when she had stared miserably out of the window, the way he had laughed when her fingers had been blackened with ink. How could she *possibly* be friends with him?

I had promised myself that I would never think about it again – Abdul and she, in that classroom, their heads coming close as if they were about to kiss. I tortured myself by replaying that moment again and again. He lifts the bottle; she holds his eye; she swallows. I knew I shouldn't, but now I couldn't stop. *Was it possible? Riya and Vikram?* I felt nothing so much as despair. The truth was that no matter how wretched he was, Vikram, like Abdul, was a sports superstar, and girls considered him, however baboon-like he appeared to me, Residency School's golden boy. In my deepest misery, I acknowledged the reality: Vikram was complete, everything that I was not. And worse, I began doubting myself, and doubting Riya. In my darkest moments, I wondered: can you ever really know someone else? No matter how hard I tried to convince myself that she would never do such a thing, those old sleepless nights slowly crept up like ugly demons.

37

I WAS WALKING Riya home from campus, a cool north wind licking past our collars, ruffling our hair. It had taken me days to build up my courage and I had planned and practised the conversation a hundred times. Now with ragged breath I began, glad that it was dark and she couldn't see my nerve-wracked face.

'Riya,' I said weakly. 'Have you and Vikram become friends?'

I must have hit an unintended chord, because she turned her head towards me and right away sensed that something was wrong.

'What on earth are you talking about?' she coolly said.

I struggled to retain my composure. 'About you and Vikram. I get it. It's fine.'

'What's fine?' she asked in a considered tone.

I was trying to act as if this conversation didn't bother me at all. I *wanted* to sound casual and nonchalant – as if I didn't really care at all. The story inside my chest, though, was something else.

'I saw you running with him the other day,' I said. 'You make a good pair.'

'He's a good runner,' she said coolly, sweeping her hair from her face.

'You guys were laughing too,' I added, almost under my breath. 'You like him.'

Riya's eyes flashed. 'So? Is something wrong with that?'

'I get it,' I gabbled, fighting to keep my voice steady. 'It makes sense. A lot more sense than you and I do, I know that.'

She stopped and, with a sigh, turned towards me. 'Really, Specs,' she said, a little gently now, 'why are you asking me all this?'

This conversation wasn't going how I had planned.

'Uh…' I murmured, rubbing my nose.

She started walking fast now, I struggled to keep up. 'I always knew you had a funny imagination,' she called over her shoulder. 'But this, this is *too* much.'

'You can tell me,' I said to her, now a little breathless from trying to keep the pace that she had set.

'Tell you what?'

'I don't know. Anything you want,' I said, my voice coming out like a strangle.

She stopped now in the middle of the road and walked up to me. She put her hand to my face. It was freezing and the cold stung my cheek.

I wasn't cutting the dignified picture I had planned. 'I thought you were mine,' I sputtered, my glasses misting. 'But you're not. And that's fine.'

'Specs,' she said slowly, her breath coming in threads of mist. 'People don't belong to each other. They belong *with* each other. I thought you of all people would understand that.'

And with that she began walking away, much too fast for me to keep up. I realized that the conversation was over and also how silly I had been. Even though I felt a little hurt that she had left me behind, a woozy relief dawned upon me. Heart of hearts, I knew that she was right and that there was nothing for me to worry about. Riya, I knew, was my girl and we were the only two people who belonged together in this world.

As Riya disappeared into the mist, her shadow far taller than she, a belligerent thought suddenly struck me so hard that I almost fell. She was mine, I knew, for the rest of our days at Residency School. But what would happen after that? Would a day come when Riya wasn't mine? And when that day came, what would happen to me?

38

ONE OF THE best things about being in the twelfth standard was that I could skip morning PT, which was always held at 6.00 a.m. when my leg was as heavy as a rock. Now I could stay up late, delving into my beloved books and then sleep in, rising just a few minutes before morning attendance.

I had big plans for my final year at Residency School. I hoped to find a clue to what my future – now less than a year away – ultimately held for me. For Riya, the answer was clear – she loved running, and that was the only thing that she wanted to do. But what was it that I was best suited for? How should I spend the life given to me? I loved mathematics more than any other subject, but what kind of future did a mathematician have? Was I better off studying medicine, engineering or economics? I devoured books, hoping to find some answers: *Great Expectations* about an orphan like me, *Catcher in the Rye* about a school that somehow seemed like mine, and *A Farewell to Arms* about a man who loved a woman as much as I did.

But so far, no book had given me the answers I was looking for and I was mired in uncertainty, trapped by the very options I had worked so hard to attain. Until now, I could sink my head into my books like an ostrich and carry on from one class to the next, but now I had to take decisions and I wasn't sure I knew how. While I was eager to learn and explore, the only place I knew was Residency School and I didn't want to step outside this ivy-clad, red-bricked world.

It was nearly two in the morning and I was halfway through Ira Trivedi's *There is No Love on Wall Street*, reading about a girl who seemed to be as confused as I was. The night was very cold and clear, and, through my window, the stars shimmered like sequins in the velvety sky. I had just opened a pack of biscuits when I heard a knock on my door. I could tell it was Ansari Sir from the two quick raps. What was he doing awake so late at night? I quickly tousled my hair and rubbed my eyes, hoping to look like I'd been just woken.

He walked into my room, smelling of the strange smells of old age, dressed in a ragged set of pyjamas. His snow-white hair stood on his head as if he had just received an electric shock.

He trained his watery, red-rimmed eyes on me, looking surprisingly helpless and vulnerable. But I knew that even at this late hour, he was as sharp as a hawk.

'Yes, sir?' I said politely, trying not to disturb my roommate.

'Have you seen Vikram?' he leaned, forward clearing his throat and peering through the glasses perched on his nose.

Vikram? Why would he think I had seen Vikram?

'Uh, no, sir.'

He continued peering at me for a second, as if distrusting my answer, suspecting I was hiding him in my tiny double room; but I knew even he could not be daft enough to think Vikram and I were friends.

He continued looking at me for a second and frowned, and then said a little vaguely, 'I can't locate him. Three others are missing too.'

'I'm very sorry, sir,' I said, not quite sure what else to say.

'Put your shoes on and get a sweater,' he said before shuffling out of my room.

I didn't have a choice but to follow him. Within moments, I found myself squeezed into the back of Ansari Sir's small Maruti car, feeling an overwhelming sense of unease. I wasn't at all worried about Vikram; I simply didn't want to be caught in the middle of unpleasantness.

Ansari Sir had also wrangled an unlucky peon and a miserable junior, who had made the mistake of staying up late to watch TV in the common room. It was this unlikely foursome that set off on what appeared to be a midnight campus hunt for Vikram and his friends.

We drove slowly around the campus, stopping at several places – the art block, the main building, a construction site where students often played hooky. The cold air was causing the windows to fog and condense, which made Ansari Sir snap and swear at the peon. This was very shocking to me: I had never in my life heard the strict and highly proper Ansari Sir utter so much as a mild curse. This, I figured, was an indication of his stress levels, which were now steadily on the rise. At each stop, the hapless junior and I tumbled out of the car, and were sent to poke futilely in the dark, while

Ansari Sir yelled out instructions and the peon scrubbed at the windows.

I could understand Ansari Sir's tension. It wasn't uncommon for boys to come back late, but it was nearly 2.00 a.m. and the middle of the week. If Vikram and his compatriots were injured, this could cast a serious blemish on Ansari Sir's record – permanently spoiling his chance for the headmastership, which he was said to dearly covet.

After thirty minutes, we reached the far end of campus, until we were beside Dhobi Ghat that survived on the largesse of the school. I was convinced that this had become a wild goose chase, and was almost on the verge of saying something to Ansari Sir – or, more likely, forcing my junior to – when we finally saw it lying there, a shimmering clue, illuminated in the moonlight.

Ansari Sir, old and weak as he was, spotted it first. He barked a command, and the peon ran to pick up the bottle and then handed it over to him. Ansari Sir sniffed at it and threw it into the bushes. We couldn't take the car inside the narrow lane, so he barked another command, and we all followed on foot. And with those few steps, it was as if the whole world had changed, and instead of grand brick buildings, cobbled streets and manicured lawns, we were now surrounded by rickety huts, dust roads and the smell of urine and cow dung.

Even though we were so close, we would never have found them in the darkness if it hadn't been for Vikram's trumpeting laugh. The sound caused me to grimace; Ansari Sir cursed softly, then beckoned us forward. We found all four of them, behind a washerman's hut, the smell of which was abominable.

Vikram lay on a ratty cot, drunk as a fish, while the other

three – along with whom I guessed was the washerman – sat on the floor next to a dying fire, attempting to play a game of cards, a bunch of crumpled-up rupee notes by their side.

Ansari Sir's voice cracked like a whip and he approached them silently, picking his way through the bottles and cigarette ends, his face as still and expressionless as a corpse. The boys looked up, startled as animals caught in a steel-tooth trap. Ansari Sir instructed Vikram to get off the cot. A senseless Vikram, saliva dripping from his mouth and down the sides of his face, clutched a bottle in his hand that contained a milky-white liquid, which I later found out was a crude form of a dangerous drug, Metalime. Despite Ansari Sir's orders, Vikram would not or could not move, and the other boys swayed badly, slurring incomprehensible words.

I had always thought Ansari Sir a faintly ridiculous figure, with his British affections and Einstein hair; a dangerous man, to be sure, but one largely to be avoided and privately derided. This night changed all that. What could have been a dangerous and unpredictable confrontation – four drunk athletes, against an ancient teacher, a tiny peon, a terrified junior and me – ended up being an orderly affair. Ansari Sir, through force of his will alone, got all boys in his car and shooed the washerman away.

For me, the sight of them drunk and drugged was so disturbing that I ended up fleeing the scene, walking back to the house in the bitter cold of this thankless night as fast as my good leg could carry me. When I reached the hostel, I realized that I was breathing very hard. My head spun with the blank faces of those boys; Ansari Sir's hard, cold incomprehensible stare; Vikram's drugged eyes rolling deep into his skull, his drunken laughter wailing like sirens in my ears. I collapsed on my bed, holding my aching leg, hoping desperately to fall asleep and to wake up and discover that this night had never happened.

39

THE FALLOUT OF Vikram's adventure in Dhobi Ghat was immediate and far-reaching. They didn't realize that I had been there, not Vikram nor the other three boys. Of course, the junior told the whole house about it, and even the peon had his two seconds of fame, fingering his moustaches and whispering furtively into boys' ears. They left my name out of it though. I suspected it was because the junior wanted all the glory for himself. I wanted to thank him for doing so, but I did not, because if he had forgotten that I had been there, I did not want to remind him now.

Ansari Sir was too preoccupied with the situation to say a word to me. He was, in fact, facing a serious dilemma. All four boys were from prominent families; all four had fathers who were alumni, who donated heavily to the school. It wouldn't be as easy to kick them out as it would have been if someone like me had been caught; and yet, were Ansari Sir to go light on them, he would face a permanent and irreparable loss of credibility. Vikram and the other boys had committed a grave crime – drinking was serious enough, but drugs, and especially a drug as serious as Metalime, was grounds for expulsion. Boys had been expelled for lesser crimes and it was almost certain that Vikram would have to leave.

Expulsion was serious for everyone, but it was an especially important event for a successful sportsman like Vikram. Expulsion meant he would be blacklisted from any state or national event, which meant that his sports career was over, not just in this school, but in any school that he ever wanted to attend.

As expected, Vikram's fall from grace caused a mad frenzy at school. Boys frantically discussed their theories about what had happened that night – it didn't help matters that after the night at Dhobi Ghat, Vikram simply disappeared. No one knew where he had gone, even the closest of his friends. Allegedly, he went straight to the infirmary, and from there to the local hospital; someone else said that he had been smuggled out in the morning, lying doped out at the back of a big black car.

Even though I usually did not care to indulge in gossip, this time even I was curious. Over the years, I had seen Vikram do plenty – cheating, drinking and smoking – on multiple occasions. But a serious drug, in the middle of the night, in his final year at school a few days before he was to be crowned prefect and bestowed the biggest honour of his life? When he had been odds-on favourite to be named head boy? To implode so spectacularly, to self-sabotage? This I did not understand. Was there something about him that I hadn't known? Something to do with his parents or their divorce? Vikram's father had remarried, and he even had a half-brother in the junior school – maybe that had caused him pain? But no matter how hard I thought about it, it was hopeless. I couldn't find the answer to this question. I suspected I was missing a crucial piece of information, something that would explain the whole thing. I was right, but it was only much later that I found out that Riya was at the heart of it all.

40

THERE ARE PERIODS in life when you earn your advancement; and there are periods when luck smiles on you. Often, these two forces are at least somewhat correlated, but you usually don't realize it at the time. So, just like that, Vikram's gravest mistake ended up being my biggest triumph, and two days after his disappearance, when the prefects were announced, Vikram, who had been a sure-shot Ashok House prefect and even a possible head boy candidate, was not on the list.

With Vikram and three other likely Ashok House prefect candidates all expelled, the impossible happened and I, Nikhil Sharma, was conferred the biggest honour of the school. A house prefect badge was bestowed upon me and with it I pledged unfaltering loyalty to Residency School.

Over the course of my life, I had mastered the ability to make myself so small that I could almost disappear. As a young boy, I would practise this, closing my eyes, shutting off the world, becoming one with the darkness. But the second I had that gilded badge pinned to my lapel, it was as if I had stepped out of the shadows and become visible to the world.

Suddenly, I was famous. The older boys in the house treated me with a cautious – if disdainful – respect; the younger ones looked at me with stars in their eyes. Even

Jeevan Singh treated me differently; I would say that it was with respect. It felt very strange to be the object of attention; all my life I had been on the sidelines, and now I was meant to be leading the squad.

And with the badge, the quiet days that I had known over my eleven years at Residency School ended as quickly as one of my dreams. The gold badge was a mark of supreme importance: many of my fellow prefects, like Mrinalini, had worked towards this honour their whole lives, but it also bore a hefty weight. Right away I was put in charge of so many things – organizing school competitions, house schedules, assemblies and attendance, writing reports for the teachers, the principal and the board, monitoring boys and supervising prep. Gone were the days of reading novels under a tree; gone were the days of bunking classes to watch Riya run; gone were the days of studying just for fun.

That said, there were certain perks. We were allowed to use the prefects' common room, which had much more comfortable sofas, and an abundance of tea biscuits. I also got my own room – for the first time in my life, my own room, all for me with a single bed, a small wooden desk and a window which looked onto the garden full of purple and magenta bougainvillaea and through which the sun poured in.

The twelve of us prefects even got to wear different uniforms than the rest of the school – blue shirts that matched the pale mountain sky, instead of the basic white-and-blue; silver-striped silk scarves with our formal uniform, instead of the standard-issue tie. The most glorious of all were the badges – enchanting golden orbs embossed with the school insignia that we proudly pinned to our chests, some boys even keeping them on while they slept. It was said that these badges were so venerated that men wore them on the lapels of their coats for the rest of their lives.

It was strange how quickly I got used to my new role as prefect. Strange, because I had never held any leadership position in this school except for chess captain. In part it was because of the respect – it came with the badge – and boys who had never noticed my existence now moved aside as I walked down the halls and looked at me with wide eyes. As for the work, I did that easily, I was after all pretty organized. I did struggle with disciplining the boys, so I tried as much as I could to avoid that job and pass it on to my fellow prefect, the football captain, to whom yelling at boys and beating them came much more naturally.

The best part of the prefectship was that Riya and I no longer had to hide our relationship. We were seniors, and fairly prominent – she a sports captain and I a prefect. The teachers simply couldn't say anything to us, and the students wouldn't dare. We could walk freely on campus, side by side, have tea together during break, share a samosa after school with nothing at all to worry about.

Looking back, I can't believe our recklessness, my recklessness. Rules meant nothing to us. Sometimes we bunked one, two or three classes together, hanging around the art block or even leaving campus through Dhobi Ghat to have a cup of tea or eat a roasted bhutta.

And we weren't the only ones. In the twelfth standard, romance seemed to bloom. Romance seemed to blood all around and boys and girls inhabited hidden corners of the school. Lovers budded and spread like wild roses and for the first time in my twelve years, Residency School began feeling like an actual co-ed school instead of an all-boys school. Shy science students finally shared their chemical bonds, sporty athletes began playing couples tennis and Mrinalini fell in love with Vikram. Many boys I knew were in love with Riya but she was only mine, and most girls, however unattractive, had at least two boys in love with her.

There was one fly in the ointment. In the few free moments I had during my busy days, I often found myself thinking about Vikram. For better or worse, Vikram's presence had been an important one in my life and now I simply could not believe that he was no longer here. I walked down the hallways of the dorm bracing myself to hear his trumpeting laugh, preparing to duck away and then as I stepped into a shadow I would remember that he wasn't there any more. During assembly I would imagine his hard grip on my shoulder as he snuck up on me from the back of the line, but then I would remember that I was a prefect now and I didn't even stand in line.

Boarding school makes you a creature of habit. Everything is orderly: your life, your schedule, your mind and when something or someone goes missing, the repercussions are magnified. And that's what it felt like with Vikram, who, despite his faults, had occupied a particular place in the Residency School system, a more prominent place than most. With him gone, many boys felt confused and lost. There was no one to take orders from, no one to adulate, no one to avoid. His spot at morning assembly – a coveted spot, by the south door – lay empty for weeks after, no one daring to step in. His 'areas', even though they occupied prime dorm real estate, were left alone – his bed by the window, with its eight shelves of storage space; the desk he had declared his own by chiselling in his name; his bathroom cubbyhole, which still contained his expensive imported gels.

But memories are short-lived at places like Residency School and one day a boy stepped into Vikram's spot in the washroom, another tumbled into his bed, someone else dumped his books on Vikram's desk and someone stole his gels. And as autumn ended and winter approached, Vikram became a vague memory in everyone's minds – everyone but mine. He had been such an integral part of my school life that with him gone, I felt an inexplicable, unpleasant void.

41

EVERY AUTUMN, RESIDENCY School held its annual athletic meet. It was the most exciting sports event of the year and over two hundred students from the junior and senior schools participated in various track and field events. The house with the most number of trophies won the Athletics Cup, the most prized trophy of our school. This was a typically gladiatorial Residency School move, pitting all the students against each other over days of races and athletic events, so that their 'best selves' would emerge.

For most of my school life, I had enjoyed the athletic meet only because I could study or read in peace while the rest of the school ran, jumped and threw things around. Riya, of course, changed that. Now I was a loyal attendant – even a bit of a fan – and I enjoyed watching it more than I ever thought I would. There was something exhilarating about the intense waiting at the start, about watching her run to the sounds of cheers and that triumphal final moment when she crossed the finish line, her torso snapping the thin white thread, her arms up by her side as if she were a bird in flight.

That year, the meet was more important than ever before. It was her last meet and she was determined to make her mark. She practised harder than I ever remember seeing her. After each run, she would sprawl loose-limbed by the tracks, spikes by her side, chewing on a blade of grass, so tired that no matter how many times I told her that we had to go, she would just say to me, 'Two minutes, Specs. I wanna rest for two more minutes.'

'But you said that seven minutes ago and I'm late for prep.'

She would just lie there, staring at a distant tree, not listening to a word I said.

I remember one such scolding in particular. It was two days before the athletic meet and she was relacing her spikes in her house colours after practice. Her face was pinched and pale, her stomach conclave.

'I don't understand why you ran so much today,' I told her with a sigh. She looked so tired these days yet she pushed herself so hard.

'I need to break all the records,' she said in a small, tired voice, putting aside a half-laced spike.

'But they're *already* yours!'

'Doesn't matter, Specs. I want to break them all anyway.'

'If only you were so ambitious about your studies,' I scolded.

Now she raised her head and rolled her eyes at me. I blushed. I didn't mean to, but I sounded like her teacher, or her father. Or maybe like both.

Then she sighed and lay down on the grass.

'It's my last year, Specs.'

'We don't know that. You still have your boards. And this time you don't have me.'

A half-laced spike came hurling at me.

'Geez, Riya,' I said as I ducked. 'Maybe you should also try the javelin throw.'

42

THE MEET ALWAYS opened with a war-like flourish, a ceremonial march-past led by the athletics captain holding the school flag. This prestigious task was usually reserved for the boys' athletic captain but because Riya had won so many state and national accolades, she led the processional that year.

It was invariably a chaotic affair. The school band would strike a merry tune, and marching squads from each house – lined in reverse order of age, from strapping seniors to squeaky thirteen-year-olds – would straggle and stumble in some kind of order, winding their way along the school grounds like a disoriented snake. That year, I got stuck leading my house in the march-past, holding the blue Ashok House flag because I was a prefect, and the other prefect was leading a special contingent of all the sports captains.

I had never participated in march-pasts, having always used my leg to explain my absence; if I had wanted to, I could have given the same excuse this year too. But I didn't want to, not when I was prefect, not when Riya was leading the parade. That's not to say I was any good though. My voice, squeaky as a rubber duck's, was not ideal for shouting out commands and I made for a sorry march-past leader.

'Specs, it really *isn't* that hard,' said Riya, who, in an ironic role reversal, was now attempting to coach me. Unfortunately, I was not as good a student as she was.

'It's simple. It's just left arm up, right leg back, right arm up, left leg back.'

'It doesn't come so naturally to me, Riya,' I complained, nearly tripping as I mixed up my left and right legs.

She sighed in exasperation. 'How can it not? It's so *easy*.'

'I guess that's kind of how I feel about quadratic equations. Easy. *Natural* for me. Hard for you.'

'Specs, don't think too much … just march,' she said with a sigh. 'If you stop dissecting, dividing and multiplying everything in that head of yours, marching will come a lot more easily.'

And she was right, so we kept at it, practising over and over again, marching to a beat, left, right, left, right. Marching behind her, it seemed to work, but when I tried it on my own, I would completely lose rhythm. Over time, I improved, but I never got good. Life just made more sense, marching behind Riya. But that I already knew.

43

THE DOME OF Residency School glowed ochre and gold in the late afternoon sun. Shreds of white cumulous cloud streaked across the sky as the house banners sparkled and snapped in the wind. The lawns shone like jade, the red tracks were perfectly chalked and hundreds – thousands – of frenzied students cheered with the full power of their lungs.

Riya marched proudly with the Residency School flag firm and high: two lions on a field of azure. She was glorious in her navy blazer with its golden captain's crest and her white skirt, which for a change had no grass stains. She wore sparkling white socks, dust-free shoes and red ribbons in her neatly plaited hair.

I, on the other hand, cut a sorry figure, barely able to hold up the heavy metal flag post, my glasses slipping down my nose. I saw her chatting with the other captains, all so strong and confident, bearing their respective flagpoles as easily as if they were toothpicks.

Riya was beaming and it seemed as if the whole world, especially the boys, were staring at her. As I watched, my heart sunk to my wobbling knees. And then we began marching; I tried my best to march to the drumbeat, at least my pounding heart was matching its beat.

I marched – 1, 2, 1, 2, 1, 2, I said over and over again. Thank God for the numbers; they made everything all right. Just as I relaxed, I tensed up again, it was my turn in front of the pavilion. I drew a deep breath, and unleashed it the way Riya said I was supposed to, with all my might. 'Ashok House, turn left!' I roared. All the boys turned their heads to the left, saluting the chief guest.

Sweating and nervous, I felt myself falling behind, the pole too slipping closer and closer to the ground. And then, somewhere on the tracks, along a serpentine turn, Riya and I found ourselves face-to-face. Just for a second, she broke the command, quickly cocking her head to the left and winking at me. My heart soared through my head and everything felt all right again.

44

I REMEMBER THE day as if it were just yesterday. The games began immediately after the march-past. The students waved their colourful flags and Scindia Pavilion seemed like a vast swarm of butterflies. As the runners took to the tracks for the 400m dash – their long limbs supple and brown, their faces chalky and drawn – the crowds went wild, chanting their names.

Then the whistle shrieked, and the runners in their crouched starting positions sprang up and took off. There wasn't much suspense because Riya had won the race even before it had begun. After all, she had held the school and state record since the tenth standard. I watched her intently because it was a pleasure watching her run. The 400 metre was her event and Riya would finish the race with the next winner not yet at the 200-metre mark.

The race started with Riya racing ahead, swift and strong like a jaguar, her legs pumping with a life of their own. You could almost hear how cleanly her spikes grabbed the dirt, almost see how the wind carried her. Somewhere near the bend of the 200-metre mark, her hair tie fell off and her hair streamed behind her, as wild as a dupatta in the wind.

She began slowing down at the 150-metre mark. From a steady sprint, she dropped to a fast jog. I assumed it was a cramp – I had seen it happen before – and with the next runner so far behind, Riya could afford to slow down. I waited for her to pick up pace but instead she became slower and slower till she was at a slow jog, head down, hands on her hips, heaving for air. I only suspected that something was wrong at the 100-metre mark, when a runner caught up with Riya, a new-found determination in her stride. At the 50-metre mark, I began hearing the susurrus of worried whispers and noticed that in the teacher's tent, B.P.'s face had turned to stone. Though she was still running, she was going very slowly, her legs wobbling, her shoulders drooping, her body moving in strange, uncoordinated jerks. Two other runners had overtaken her by now, but if Riya sped up, even now she could win the race.

It all happened as if in slow motion and I stood there, very still. I saw B.P. run to the sidelines and stand there waiting for her. He would let her finish the race: this is the athlete's ethos, this would be the right way. She ran very, very slowly, her spikes digging into the ground and when the lead runner burst through the thread, winning the race, not a single cheer went up in the stands. Riya ran behind everyone, barely able to finish, and right after she crossed the finish line, she collapsed on to the ground. Lots of people fainted during races, but something just felt so wrong about this. B.P. ran to her, lifted her up as easily as if she were a rag doll and sprinted towards the medical tent with her in his arms. Behind him I noticed a thin red trail of Riya's blood.

Part 2

45

RIYA DIDN'T COME to school for a few days after the race, and I was worried sick. But she got annoyed with me when I tried to fuss over her, pale-faced and thin.

'Everything okay?' I asked as she lay still on the sofa at her house.

'Yes, yes, I'm fine,' she replied in a wisp of a voice. But she didn't look fine. Her face looked thin and exhausted like she was tired, or ill or maybe both.

I fretted and twittered like a bird. 'Anything I can do to make you feel better?'

'No, I told you, I am fine. It's just low blood pressure – it happens to runners all the time.'

She didn't say anything after that and I knew from her tone that the conversation was done. I got up, collected my things and left for prep.

Things went on like that for a few days, till one evening, at around 9.00 p.m., as I was settling in with my books, a junior knocked on my door and told me I had a call. I was surprised – no one had ever called me on the Ashok House telephone. It turned out to be Riya, calling from the train station, saying that she was headed to Delhi with B.P. for a race. I was surprised. Was she well enough to go? She replied in a flustered tone that her father was with her and I had nothing to worry about. I heard the whistle of a train in the distance and the rattle of the tracks, and she told me hastily that she had to go. And then she was gone. Even though I was confused, I didn't think much of it. She left so often for meets that while this sudden departure struck me as odd, it was nothing out of the ordinary.

A day passed, and then another. Before I knew it, a whole week had slipped by and I had no news from her. She had been gone longer than usual but I told myself that I had nothing to worry about. She was gone for a meet, her father was with her and things were absolutely fine, she had said so herself. Yet I couldn't help but worry. She had left so suddenly right after her fall.

What made it worse was that I had no way of getting in touch with her. I began hanging around outside Ansari Sir's office in the evening, hoping for a phone call. I became so desperate that once when I thought I heard the phone ring, I rushed in only to have him look at me oddly, as the phone sat quietly on the hook.

One evening as I sat glumly in my room, having almost given up hope, a peon came to tell me that I had a call. I leapt to my feet and rushed down the hall in my socks.

Riya's voice was weak and tired. I should have known then that something was wrong but I was so absorbed in my own desire to hear her voice that I didn't realize a thing.

'Hi, Specs.'

'Riya, where have you been?' I said, suddenly angry after days of waiting and worrying.

'Specs, are you *angry* with me?' she said finally with a laugh.

I never got angry with her, even when she had messed up the easiest of sums. I even more rarely called her by her name.

'Uh, yeah … I mean, no…' I cleared my throat so I would not sound like a fool. 'Why didn't you call me all these days?'

'I'm sorry. I forgot the number.'

Typical Riya. She had never had a head for numbers.

'I was worried about you.'

'I … I know … I'm sorry,' she said, her voice sounding very far away.

'Is everything okay?'

'Everything is *fine*, Specs. You worry too much.'

I heard an officious woman's voice in the background, and a lot of clattering. Where was she?

'I…'

Before I could finish, she cut me off.

'I gotta go, Specs,' she said in a hurry, and hung up.

'Miss you,' I completed the sentence to the plastic phone. I sat in Ansari Sir's chair for a moment, staring at the receiver, holding it for a moment and letting her voice sink into my soul.

Thankfully, I couldn't dwell on my misery, as I would have in the past. I was on my feet from morning until night, looking after two hundred boys, adjudicating disagreements, meting out punishment, organizing games rotas. I barely even had any time to study and for the first time in my life, my grades slipped. But I knew that I could pull up at the end of the year. It was only the boards that mattered in the twelfth standard, and teachers tended to cut prefects a lot of slack. I tried to get through my days trying my best not to obsess over her. But no matter how hard I tried and no matter how much I ignored it, I missed her all the time. Seeing her felt to me as necessary as oxygen, as fundamental as air. At least I still had my dreams and no one – not Ansari Sir, not Principal Sir, not even Riya herself – could take those away from me. In the night, utterly exhausted, I would close my eyes and there she was, waiting for me on the other side.

46

I KNEW IT was late because the morning sun was strong on my face, and though there were a million things to get done, I didn't want to open my eyes. My dream was as beautiful as a dream could be. She was running on a fluffy white cloud, in the background was the crimson sky and there I was, running as gracefully as her, right by her side. My legs pumped easily, matching her stride for stride. It was all so real that I could feel my thumping heart.

Then, suddenly, my door flew open with a bang and I was jolted out of my reverie. For a second, squinting against the stabbing sun I thought I was still asleep and then in the next, I thought that I was seeing a ghost.

There he stood before me, thinner, harder than when I had seen him last, wearing a pair of jeans, tight around his muscled legs, and a black T-shirt which clung to his chest. He stood in my doorway, staring at me blankly, looking at the room for a long time, not saying a word to me. For a second I was thankful for my poor eyesight: I might be mistaken, it might not be him. Then he spoke, and I recognized that voice without an iota of doubt.

'You know, Oily, this room, it's cosy, it's meant to be mine.'

With that, he walked away, slamming the door behind him. I blinked stupidly, still fuzzy with sleep, wondering how this could possibly be real.

The official story was that Vikram had returned, his expulsion revoked so that he could lead the Residency School hockey team in the national championships, which people said they couldn't win without him. Maybe there was some truth to it, but it wasn't the entire truth. All sorts of theories were hatched and floated – Vikram's dad had used his influence over the board to get him back; someone else said that the chief minister had made a special call; Mrinalini stupidly insisted that she knew for a fact that the prime minister had intervened.

Whatever it was and however he had done it, it didn't matter because he was back – back in his uniform, back in his bed, back in his spot in the sun during line-up. Vikram, who was meant to be gone forever, had returned and now it was like he had never even left.

Seeing him again was really like something out of a horror film and I passed the next few days in dread, trying my best to avoid him and his gang, who had gravitated back to him as naturally as the planets around the sun. I took to lurking around Ansari Sir's office even when I didn't have any work, simply to avoid Vikram. But Ansari Sir, tired of my endless questions about dress code policy and school trip protocols, promptly asked me to leave. But, in the way he paced the room and kept asking me to bring in boys so he could rap their palms with steel, I could tell that even he was worried. He disliked Vikram almost as much as I did and was furious, and probably a little scared too, that he was back.

As for Vikram, without the prefecture to compete for, his behaviour was even worse than before. He bunked curfew and smoked openly. He bullied boys with a viciousness like never before. More than anything, he began challenging my authority deliberately, trying to make my life as difficult as possible.

I felt a growing sense of unease. This house belonged to me as much as any other boy – maybe even *more* than other boys because I was prefect. But after he had returned, everything felt different; or rather, it felt the same, the way it used to be. I felt that he was always watching me with those beady eyes like ominous stars, always thinking about the badge that I was wearing that should have been his. I began looking over my shoulder, keeping my head low and even though I was the highest authority in this house, I began feeling like some new junior school boy.

But no matter how much I avoided him, seeing him was inevitable. At evening line-up when I did attendance, he would call in a shrill voice pretending to be a girl, 'Check me, Oily, check me.' This caused a gale of laughter and I looked like a fool. And then he hissed at me through clenched teeth as I ignored him and went through the line. I pretended not to hear him but the truth was that I, a prefect, was quaking with fear.

Throughout all this, I wished desperately that she were here, and every evening I cycled over to her house, hoping that, by some stroke of luck, she may just be back. But the little house lay abandoned, and only Jeevan Singh's rusty bike stood parked outside the gate.

47

SUNDAY EVENING BEGAN uneventfully with the usual sundry problems – boys who had left campus and hadn't reported back, someone sneaking in chicken which he was eating in bed, boys trying to get out of duties as weekly schedules were made.

I went to bed late and though I was bone-tired, I simply couldn't sleep. I kept turning fitfully in bed, thinking of random things, straining my ears to catch the ring of a phone call that I knew would not come. The discomfort chewed into my stomach till the wee hours of the morning, when finally I fell into a restless slumber, yearning for her to come.

But that night she did not. Instead, I was jolted awake when I felt cold, rough fingers tighten around my neck. He grabbed my collar hard and I heard the painful rip. It was pitch dark and I couldn't see a thing, but I could feel them – so many of them – crowded into my little room.

'My glasses,' was the only thing I said, my voice scarcely a whisper, and then a piece of cloth – I later discovered that it was my own collar – was shoved into my mouth.

They dragged me into the toilets, a herd of muscled arms and legs, talking in loud whispers, their voices hard with hate. They tied my arms and my feet, and all I could do was squirm like a soundless worm, the piece of cloth still stuffed into my mouth. I heard one zip open and then the next and then they all took turns urinating onto my face. In my worst nightmare, they came after me with hockey sticks and cricket bats, but they did none of that tonight. They just kicked me and pissed on me, and someone joked that he wished he had to shit.

I heard him over all of them, that cruel voice, that muffled laugh. The others, I couldn't be entirely sure of who they were, but I was pretty sure that amongst them were boys who had invited me to eat with them, whom I had tutored, whose friendship I thought I had won.

They left me locked up in a bathroom and I lay there, my face at the bottom of a dirty toilet, thinking one thing throughout it all. Riya. Riya. Why had she not come? Many hours later – I couldn't be sure exactly how long – I heard sounds that moved briskly, but I couldn't understand anything, the pain in my head had become a loud drum. I tried hitting the door with my feet, though I was so weak that I barely made a sound.

I felt an arm on my leg and a spark of pain in my head as a boy lifted my head out of the toilet. I finally opened my eyes. He stood there staring at me, his mouth a horrified 'o'. He didn't immediately help me or even say anything; instead he ran away as I lay on the floor of the toilet, fighting the pain and moaning like a girl. The boy returned with three other boys, who whispered amongst themselves and dragged me out, untied my hands and my feet and took my collar out of my mouth.

By this time, boys were streaming into the toilet and I got up, slowly, painfully, unsteadily. My head was throbbing, my leg was on fire and my chest hurt like a beast. So much for the nightmares that were filled with gore and blood. This, what they had done to me, was so much worse. Without saying a word, without looking at any of them I limped back to my room and slowly shut the door. I lay down on the scarred wood floor, covered with blood and piss, listening to the steady sound of the rain.

48

TYPICALLY, AFTER HER long trips, Riya would come back and chatter nonstop – about the races she had won, the people she had met, the places she had been to, her gold medals on display. But today she just sat there on the steps of the verandah, staring absentmindedly into space.

I remember I was telling her about Vikram's return when in the midst of a sentence, I looked at her and she was gazing at the sinking sun. She didn't even notice that I had stopped talking until I tapped her lightly on her shoulder, bringing her back from wherever she had gone.

'What's wrong?' I knew that something clearly was.

'Nothing, Specs,' she murmured. 'I'm a bit tired. It's been a long trip.'

I wanted to say something, but I did not. When she was tired, she got easily annoyed and she had just come back after so many days. So we sat there, in silence, on the steps of her house, the dimming light hiding her face like a shroud. A light bulb came on in the garden and the light on her body shifted subtly, seeming now as if a spell was radiating from her. I was filled with an unexpected, soaring joy – here she was, finally in front of me in real human form. She was paler than usual, and there were dark circles under her eyes, but to me she was still the most beautiful girl in the world. Seeing her, all the wounds I had inside and out seemed to magically heal.

In the distance, I heard the bells toll. It was 6.30 p.m., time for evening prep that I had to supervise. Reluctantly, I heaved myself to my feet, and once again, for the thousandth time, I missed the old days when all I had to care about was Riya and me.

But Riya caught hold of my hand and looked up at me, a strange clear look in her eyes.

'I have something to tell you,' she said, in an unusual tone.

I looked at her, now uncomfortable, waiting for her to break the silence. All sorts of unpleasant thoughts were beginning to run through my mind. I pictured Vikram gloating as he stood so close to her, like the day he had when I had cycled past. I remembered the way he had smiled at her and how she had laughed and flipped her hair.

My mind was now a tornado of thoughts. *Vikram and Riya. Could it possibly be?* I felt my head go light and spin around and I was back in the bathroom again, my head in the toilet and piss in my mouth. I was back again, standing by the window, looking through the grills, and Abdul was bending towards Riya. Feeling faint, the clouds moving like waves, I sat down, almost missing the step. I held my head in my hands, fragments of a prayer that I had once learnt as a little boy coming to my lips.

'I'm sick,' she said in a hoarse whisper.

I looked up and blinked.

She just stared at the ground in front of her. She was going to tell me that something had happened between them. That she loved Vikram. I continued staring dumbly at her.

'I'm really sick, Nikhil,' she whispered again.

'Will you stop saying that? And just tell me the truth? If you like Vikram and not me…'

I could feel the tears welling up now in my leaky eyes. Thank god I wore glasses that could hide my stupid tears.

'I'm about to die,' she said without looking me in the eye.

The wind was up and a gentle rain pattered on the roof of the porch. The smell of the sodden, decaying forest was so thick it almost suffocated me. But I didn't move. I just sat there outside her house on the damp steps until Jeevan Singh hobbled out with a cup of hot tea. Riya had gone inside some time ago, but I just sat there with the chipped blue glass in my hand until it got cold.

Part 3

49

IT WAS JUST like Riya to tell me exactly the way that it was. No comforting words, no gentle lies, nothing at all to cover the sores. She had cancer and not just any ordinary cancer, but a rare small cell lung cancer. There had been signs – stomach aches, headaches and no periods for six months. It turned out that her biggest strength had been her biggest downfall. She was an athlete, and athletes were used to pain and she hadn't paid attention to the symptoms until it was too late. She hadn't thought to tell anyone: not her coach, not her father, not even me. She had fought through it, thinking that it would eventually get better, like her pain always did. But this pain didn't get any better. It only grew worse till she was forced to take attention during the athletic meet.

The fact was that Riya had won races and medals with tumours growing in both lungs. I wondered how much she must have suffered: her lungs could apparently do only half of what a normal person's could. But I suppose I shouldn't have been surprised, because that was Riya for you. I thought of my own leg and how much the pain bothered me. Just went to show what she really was, and what I really was.

By the time she found out, the doctors said that there was nothing that they could do. The cancer had already spread to her bones, her spine, her brain, to her blood. There was no cure, no operation; chemotherapy, apparently, would do more harm than good. They said the cancer was terminal, which meant that Riya was going to die. Apparently, she had anywhere from a month to three months to live. They said that the only thing left to do now was to pray. I knew that Riya had never said a prayer in her life.

I was no stranger to death. My parents, after all, were dead. But Riya? *Dying*? I simply could not imagine it, couldn't believe it, couldn't fathom it. It had to be a lie or a mistake. Riya was the most alive person I knew.

In the days that followed, I simply checked out. I couldn't absorb her words. I couldn't absorb anything, not even math. I felt like I was stuck in a bad dream, a zombie at the end of the world, the final survivor in a global apocalypse, stumbling around the verdant little world of Residency School, wondering when I would wake up and when this whole nightmare would end.

She stopped coming to school almost immediately. If people wondered where she was, no one asked me. I went to see her every day, shirking all the prefect responsibilities that were once so important to me. I would finish school and go to her house, where I would always find her sitting out on the steps. Though she no longer came to school, she always wore the Residency School games uniform – blue track pants, white sports T-shirt and a thick blue jacket which hung loosely around her body, hiding every one of her curves.

Our meetings were filled with awkward silences, not the lightness and laughter of the past. I didn't believe that she had cancer, but she insisted that it was true. The results could have been someone else's – mistakes happened all the time. Exams marks were often mixed up, all it took was the teacher entering the wrong marks in the register, so why couldn't this happen with cancer test results? When I told her my theory, she just denied it, staring into the distance, absently rubbing one foot behind her calf, an old runner's trick to loosen the feet.

Although I knew she needed me, I suddenly felt very distant from her. I felt like I was transported back to the tenth standard, where I sat next to her, so nervous that I could barely speak. But at least back then we had numbers and formulae and theorems to fill up the silence, which now became worse every day. I wished so hard, squinting my eyes so tight that I thought they would burst, that we could go back to those days, to the beginning, and start all over again. But when I opened my eyes, everything remained exactly the same.

To make things worse, with Vikram back, my briefly peaceful dorm life had come to an end. It transpired that Vikram blamed me – and not the drugs – for being stripped of his badge, and all sorts of rumours began floating about. Some said that I had snitched him out to Ansari Sir; others said I had led the search party; someone even said I had given him the drugs. I ignored it all as best as I could – after all, there was little else that I could do – but the rest of the house didn't, and everyone in my house, even those whom I had considered my quasi-friends, began ignoring me or passing snide remarks. Even my former roommate couldn't look me in the eye.

I didn't talk to Riya about what was going on at school, because the last thing I wanted to do was to dump my problems on her. It was only later that I realized that this is exactly what I should have done. When I eventually did start talking to her about my problems, I realized how inconsequential they were when you only had thirty days to live.

50

A NEW HIGHWAY has been built on the foothills, but the precarious journey remains unchanged, the same hairpin bends, the same blind turns, the same uphill climb on fourth gear. As a kid, I had always had a hard time with this part. It was almost a ritual: throwing up at Milestone 63 and then spending the rest of the trip sucking on a lemon, clutching my pounding head.

Even though I am nauseous, I am as enchanted as I had always been by how beautiful this part of the journey was. The landscape changes suddenly and the tall skinny trees are replaced with thick, fragrant pines, the rounded hills sharpening into majestic mountains which merge into the steel-blue clouds.

Looking at the misty mountains, veiled by their cloak of clouds, I realize that however much I hate my memories, I love this dramatic windswept vista. The mountains, I realize, will always be a part of me, and I tell myself that I will bring Meeta and my son here this year. I purposely do not reflect on how empty my promises have been of late.

I stop now next to a small tea stall made of tarpaulin and steel sheets, where, right on mark, I throw up my frugal lunch. I smile when I see the lemons and bags of salt on sale and I buy some, remembering how hard the climb was that began from here.

51

SCARED NOW OF death, I was no longer scared of him. I needed to talk to someone, to understand what was happening to me – understand what was happening to her – and he was the only option I had.

'Sir, do you have a minute?' I asked B.P.

B.P. was home, sitting in his summer chair. There was no book of poems in his hand. Instead, he looked out of the window with little interest in his eyes. I figured this is where Riya got that habit of hers.

He looked at me confused – I rarely spoke to B.P., let alone looked him in the eye. He was sports master and Riya's father; he was not an ordinary man to me, but a giant, an immortal, and I was astonished to see how tired and haggard he looked.

'Yes,' he said after a second. 'Come. Come sit down.'

I didn't hesitate or filter myself. The words just burst from me.

'Is it true? How is this possible?' I asked even before I reached the chair.

'I'm afraid that it is,' he said, his face a rock, not displaying a thing.

I suddenly felt very unbalanced and though I hadn't earlier wanted to sit down, now I needed to.

'You mean…'

'Yes,' he said, cutting me off and I was thankful that he had stopped me from saying the word.

'But it makes no sense.'

He took a deep breath and closed his eyes.

We sat there in strained silence, and from far away I heard the echoes of students at play. It was games time, and I knew that B.P. ought to be out on the field with his team. Instead, he sat here, his grief hanging around the house like a dense fog.

I wanted to get up and leave, but where could I possibly go? The thought of going back to the house and dealing with mundane problems of boarding school life – detention, homework, exit passes – filled me with dread. I never thought that this could happen, but at this point in time, B.P. was the only person on campus I wished to speak to.

I heard a distant bell ring and tentatively I rose to leave, but B.P. held his arm out, motioning for me to sit down.

'You know…' he said finally, his voice trailing off. 'Her mother, she died of the same thing.'

I sat there looking at him, the expression on my face full of silent questions.

'The doctors had warned us twelve years ago that this disease was genetic and that there was a high chance that Riya would get it. We ran all the tests, but there was no sign at all, not at that time, and not in the years following her mother's death. The funny thing is,' he continued with the faintest quiver in his voice, 'they also told us that she had weak lungs and that she would never be able to run. After she became a runner, and such good one too, I never worried about what the doctor's had said … not even once.'

B.P. had never said so much to me at one time, or ever. I sat there, unblinking, listening to him. Only one strange thought seemed to swirl around my mind. Her mother – she must have died the same year as mine.

'Now, they say she has a month, maybe three…'

I swallowed. 'Maybe more?'

'Maybe,' said B.P. with a strange look on his face, which I only later realized was extreme fear.

'Is there anything I can do?' I asked stupidly.

B.P. looked at me sadly. He looked at me for a long time. His eyes seemed to focus slightly. 'No. No, son. There is nothing anyone of us can do.'

I wanted to ask him so many questions, to talk to him some more, but I said nothing. He said nothing and both of us just sat there for ages, saying nothing at all.

Finally, when the light had faded and the crickets had replaced the evening birds and I had missed evening line and maybe even prep, he sighed heavily and waved me out of the door.

52

IT'S ONLY NOW that I am a father that I realize what B.P. must have gone through. Back then though, I was oblivious to anyone's pain but my own. I was so involved in my own terror, my own shock, my own grief, that what B.P. may have been feeling as her father, after already having lost Riya's mother, never really struck me. I could only think about myself, about how cruel the world was, first taking away my parents and now her, wondering why I couldn't just die and put an end to all the misery.

As I scale the dizzying heights of the mountain, fighting to keep my focus, looping the car round and round, so many thoughts swirl in my head. When my son was a baby, I remember how he scraped his knee and we had rushed him to ER; how when he had a bad cough, we worried that he would choke and die. The fear that a parent feels for his child is one of the most powerful emotions in the world, and though I loved Riya with all my being, and she was the centre of my universe, the pain that I had felt was incomparable to a father's pain. This I did not realize, I could not realize, till I became a father myself.

I am brought back to the world by the ringing of my phone. My wife's name flashes on the screen. I take a deep breath, clear my throat and pick up the phone. I make an effort to be calm: the Nikhil she knows, not the Specs I have been so careful to conceal.

'It's a girl,' she says calmly.

'A girl,' I say slowly. It is hitting me bit by bit, not all at once. 'We're having a girl.'

'Yes, a girl,' she says, warm now, smiling in her voice.

A girl, I think, a little girl. I do not know if it is the wind, the nausea, the drive, or something else, but I feel one little tear make its way down my face.

53

I CYCLED DOWN to Riya's house in the evening during games time, leaving behind the cries of victory and the screams of play, cycling closer towards cruel tragedy. But today she wasn't there, sitting on the steps, waiting for me. I rang the doorbell. Jeevan Singh opened the door, a sad, toothless smile on his wrinkled face.

'Riya?' I ask.

He gave me a fierce look, grumbling that even though she was supposed to rest, she had left half an hour ago in the direction of the school. One tiny benefit of Riya's illness was that Jeevan Singh had become somewhat less acrimonious towards me.

I thanked him and hopped back on my bike. I had come from the school, but hadn't seen her on the way. I had a strong suspicion of where she may be. At first I thought that I may have been wrong, because I didn't see her right away. But then I spotted a little lump on the ground, lying on the side of the track on her back, her face towards the nougat-coloured sky. My heart almost jumped out of my chest and though we weren't allowed to bring cycles on the track, I rode as fast as I could to her side.

She heard me approaching and slowly got to her feet, red mud clinging to her white shirt.

'I knew you'd come.'

'Then why didn't you just tell me?' I said, gasping for air.

'What happened, Specs? You cycled too fast?' she said with a grin.

I was slightly mollified; no matter what, at least I could still make her laugh.

'What are you doing here?' I asked, letting the bike fall carelessly to the grass.

'What do you think?' she replied lightly, brushing her shorts.

I goggled at her. 'We need to talk.'

'What's there to talk about?'

'I don't know. Cancer maybe?'

She shrugged. 'I guess we all die, right?'

'Not like this … and not so soon.'

Riya brushed the hair from her face. 'Your parents died in a car crash. That was more sudden than this. My mom died of cancer too.'

I was still catching my breath and now I felt a cramp creeping from my stomach to my chest. I knelt down, hands on my knees, head towards the ground like Riya had taught me to do.

'Our parents were thirty. You are sixteen. Plus, you're *not* dying,' I said.

'But I am.'

My voice slightly cracked. 'But you're *not*.'

And then after a pause, seeing that I had gotten no reaction out of her, I stood up and looked her in the face. 'You're making me angry.'

'*I'm* making *you* angry?' she teased.

'I'm serious.'

But she didn't take me seriously at all. 'Can you crack my toes,' she says, kicking off her shoes.

'This is no time for cracking your toes!' I said, trying to sound fierce.

'It is though. They hurt,' she said, plonking down on the ground.

'No.'

Though she was ill and tired, her eyes still sparkled. She pursed her lips and smiled.

'Please?' she asked simply.

I melted in an instant, an ice cube in the sun. 'Fine,' I sighed, settling on the ground next to her.

And there I was, pulling and cracking her toes as she lay on her back and stared into the sky.

'I don't feel … anything,' she mused.

'But I've already cracked two,' I said, her foot in my lap.

'I don't mean the toes. I meant about dying.'

'Oh.'

'I mean, some part of us would know, right, if we were just going to die?'

'I'm not sure,' I said, not fully understanding what she was trying to say.

'Did you know with your parents? That they were going to die?'

'I don't think so, but I was so young. Did you know with your mom?' I asked tentatively.

'I think…' she said, frowning, doubt in her voice.

'If something were to happen to you, I think I would know,' I said.

'No, you wouldn't.'

'Yes, I would,' I firmly replied.

That shut her up. Because she knew it was true. For a while we sat, her toes cracked, her feet still in my lap. Then she sprang up from the track in a way that I would never be able to and stretched her back, two quick cracks from side to side. I thought for the thousandth time: *how could this be true when she looks so well.*

'Specs, you'll time me, right?' she said, tossing me the stopwatch.

'What're you doing?' I asked, surprised.

'Practising, what else?' she replied.

I was appalled. 'Isn't that dangerous?'

'For you, maybe,' she laughed, trotting off to the starting blocks.

I could argue with her but I knew that it was pointless.

She took position, digging her bare feet in the ground, poised on her fingertips. I hunkered in my usual spot beneath the scoreboard, the flimsy plastic stopwatch ticking in my hand.

'Ready?' she called faintly.

I completed the ritual: 'Go.'

She began as she usually did, bending her head down low, touching the earth with her hand and then bringing it to her head. And then she started slowly but swiftly, her mouth a little open, her tongue touching the tips of her teeth. She hadn't even gone a hundred metres when I saw her flailing, her arms and legs bobbling out of sync. No one else would have noticed, but I knew her gait like the back of my hand and I knew that she wasn't going to make her time. She reached the 200-metre turn when she should have been streaking across the finish line. She had run faster with a 101 fever, a sprained ankle or a bleeding sore on her foot. It was her slowest 400-metre attempt that I had ever timed. She crossed the finish line, white in the face, her hands on her tiny waist, breathing in sharp pained gasps, breathing more heavily than I had ever seen before.

'Time?' she managed, approaching me with a lurching walk.

'Two minutes thirty,' I said in a shaky voice, cutting it by twenty-five seconds, my heart beating as fast as hers.

She stood there for a few seconds, bent over, catching her breath, gulping air.

'Liar,' she finally said in a breathless voice.

She grabbed the stopwatch from my hand, looked at the incriminating time and then threw the stopwatch into the air with as much force as she could.

'Good riddance,' I said.

'Yeah,' she agreed softly and then sat down in the middle of the tracks.

Maybe it was seeing her time or watching her struggle to run just 400 metres, but as I sat with her in the sand, it struck me – really struck me – that Riya was actually sick, really truly sick, and that there was a real possibility that she would die. Till now, I had been in denial. I had entertained all kind of private hopes – Riya was making this all up and it was some cruel joke; Riya was trying to bunk school; the doctors had misdiagnosed her and they would call and tell her that they had made a mistake; or simply that Riya was sick and that she would get better, the way that sick people do. But now, for the first time, I began wondering if all of this were actually true.

'I'm all in,' she gasped, still breathless, rubbing her legs, laughing over at me. 'I'm done for.'

I knew then that it had struck her too.

I didn't say anything to her but we sat like that for a while in the dimming light. I could feel her shivering in the settling cold so I took off my sweater and handed it to her. But she didn't put it on, she just held it in her lap, absently rubbing the fabric.

'Are you scared?' I asked.

'Mostly no,' she answered with a shrug.

'I would be,' I slowly said.

'I don't know. I ... just don't feel a thing,' she said, her voice trailing off. 'I guess some races you can't win.'

'Life isn't exactly a race,' I said quietly.

'I know, Specs. I didn't mean it like that. It's just that you win some races, and you lose some, but you accept them all the same way. That's the only way I can really think about things right now. Good things happen, bad things happen and I guess you just accept them all in the same way.'

'This is not just a good thing or a bad thing. This is a *matter-of-life-and-death* thing.'

She gazed up at the sky and continued, as if I hadn't spoken. 'You know, Specs, I wasn't always as good at running as I am right now. Earlier, I would always think about the finish line, about the bends and turns that would get me there. About all the steps I had left to take. Then one day, I changed that, and I started thinking of *just* running, not of winning or of losing but of really feeling every step, and putting in my best. And that's when I became really good. That's what I'm kind of doing, thinking not of tomorrow, but of now. One step at a time.'

Even though I wanted to tell her that she had to fight, that she couldn't just give up on life, I sat quietly contemplating her words, trying to understand if she had a point.

We sat there for a long time, not talking, the night settling down around us, first violet then blue then silvery black. We both gazed at our favourite stars winking brightly at us, the Pegasus, the Shepard and the Little Bear. We were looking at the same sky but seeing such different things. The stars were never – before or since – brighter to me than they were that night.

54

'CAN I GO to the doctor's with you?'

'Why, Specs? Don't tell me you want to be a doctor now.'

'Um, no,' I lied. 'I just thought that maybe I could go with you. It gives me a chance to bunk classes too.'

To be honest, I had given it a thought. If I became a doctor, my life would have purpose. I would find a cure for cancer and make sure that Riya was all right.

'Bunking?' She laughed warmly. 'Since when do you bunk?'

When she saw that I was serious, she stopped smiling and studied me, like my face was a particularly interesting running track, and then she patted my arm. 'I guess it should be fine. I'll just ask Papa.'

I didn't mention that going with her had been B.P.'s idea in the first place. Riya had been seeing a doctor at the local hospital for blood tests and other medical things and when I had come over looking for her the other day, he had told me, not looking up from the book that he was holding, that she was at the hospital and that one of these days if I too could go with her.

These trips of hers – though time-consuming – gave me some hope. As long as she kept seeing doctors and going to the hospital, it seemed like there was at least a small chance of finding a cure.

So for the first time in my twelve years at Residency School, I bunked a full day of classes to go to the hospital.

Riya had told me what she obviously considered the most relevant information about Dr Chopra: his breath didn't smell, he didn't talk too much and that he was 'relaxed', although I wasn't sure if that was a quality that I wanted in Riya's doctor.

In real life, Dr Chopra was even more pleasant than Riya had made him out to be. He was friendly, greeting me with a smile and Riya with a pat on her back. He had snow-white hair, powdery skin and light grey eyes that looked like a monsoon cloud about to burst. He immediately noticed the golden badge pinned to my chest and congratulated me for being a prefect. He added with a chuckle that while he was never good enough to have been a prefect himself, a cousin of his had done the family proud by becoming the head boy.

Riya was led away by a short plump nurse for tests. While she was gone, Dr Chopra let me sit in his office, a crowded room where patients came and went. In one lull between patients, he offered me tea and then settled back into his chair and asked me gently if I had any questions for him.

Did I have questions? I had questions. I couldn't sleep, I had so many questions. For so many nights, questions had buzzed round and round in my head like the fireflies that the junior school boys caught in jars, and there was one in particular that I felt was slowly driving me mad.

'Why her, doctor?' I asked, hoping that he could explain why of all the sixteen-year-olds in the world, why this had to happen to my girl.

He looked at me for a long moment, sipping his chai. Then he smiled kindly and told me in his patient voice, 'It is very unusual, of course,' and then asked, 'You've studied biology?'

'Yes, sir.'

'Then you will easily understand. It all comes down to one cell in the body amongst billions of cells. Each cell is supposed to die when its time comes, but a small genetic defect produces one bad cell that refuses to leave. That one bad cell grows, and divides uncontrollably, producing more and more bad cells. This army of bad cells has no respect for tissue boundaries and they invade areas of the body where they have no right to go. Eventually, our whole body goes to war against the army of bad cells, but it's a war that's already won. Or lost. The bad cells are invincible, and they can never die.'

I swallowed. 'Is that cancer?'

He nodded. 'That starts just about now.'

I pictured one malicious leukocyte multiplying furiously, taking over her whole body. I felt a stab of anger and clenched my fists.

The doctor continued in his placid voice: I got the impression he gave bad news often and it must usually be in this tone. 'The bad cells invade the whole body with uncontrolled growth and at the end of the war between the good cells and the bad cells, even the very strong bad cells are in a sorry state. They lose all normal functions like accurate DNA replication, control over the cell cycle and interaction with other cells.'

Dr Chopra smiled sadly, shaking his head. He blew on his tea. 'It's all about a bad cell that just doesn't want to die. And one day, when the situation becomes terrible, the soul decides to stop the war and turn the master switch off. That is how it ends.'

I pondered over the doctor's explanation for a long time as I waited for Riya to return. He left to attend other patients while I remained on that small plastic chair for what felt like forever, thinking about that one bad cell that refused to die.

55

'THE FUNNY THING, Specs, is that I didn't even know where the lungs were before all this. I thought they were in the stomach. Because my coach always used to tell me to breath from my stomach.'

That finally brought a smile to my face. I remembered explaining to her, before the tenth-standard board exam, where each organ was, and drawing in the balloon lungs above the mango-shaped liver. I had told her to pay attention since this was a sure-shot board question but Riya had just shrugged.

'That was on our boards, you know.'

'Too bad I didn't have cancer then,' she said with a twisted little smile. 'I could have got that one right.'

'I don't want you speaking like this,' I said and turned my head away.

We were lying on the grass in Riya's garden on an unusually warm afternoon, the sweet smell of grass and pine wafting in the air. We had shed our thick woollen sweaters and they were rolled up in balls under our heads. Above us, the sky, like the ocean, stretched blue and endless and deep, behind us hunkered the steadfast mountains, blue and green and grey, always the same but always changing, one day like fury, on another the epitome of calm. As the breeze kissed my cheeks, I wanted to forget everything just for a moment and lose myself in the infinite sky.

But Riya wouldn't let me forget, not even for a second. She joked about her cancer often, which I knew I was supposed to find funny, but really just made me want to cry.

Enough was enough. I hated it when she spoke so morbidly. So I decided, on an impulse, that today I would protest, leap up on my feet and storm away, like I had often see her do. But in my energetic effort, my glasses slipped off my face and landed in a puddle.

Riya burst out laughing, while I just stood there, spectacle-less.

'Oh, Specs, drama doesn't suit you!' she said, raising her arm, beckoning me to come back.

'This day isn't going to last forever,' she continued as I stood there like a fool, glasses in my hand. 'Papa will be back soon.'

She was right, she always was. Plus, what was I trying to prove to a girl who was so ill. So I picked up my sweater, rolled it up again and lay under the strong mountain sun, knowing I would be nursing sunburns tonight. Riya, on the other hand – even with the yellowness of illness – would turn a beautiful, golden-brown.

'Some people have much less time than me, you know,' she said, looking up into the powdery sky. 'Ma had less. She had two weeks to live after she found out.'

I hitched myself up on one elbow, wanting to look her in the face, but she had turned over, looking away from me and at the mountains instead.

'She had been sick for a while, but no one knew. They thought it was jaundice. I remember her going to the hospital and then never coming back.'

Riya never spoke about her mom, like I never spoke about mine. Only once had she shown me a photo: a hazy photo of a young woman, her sari blowing in the wind, her most striking feature, her wild curly hair.

'Even though I don't remember her, I know I loved her,' she said quietly.

Riya looked uncomfortable. It wasn't like her to talk about feelings. That was mostly my role; and when I did, she would laugh and say, 'You think too much, Specs. It must be all that chess.'

'I'm luckier than her at least, aren't I, Specs?' she said stiffly, turning around, looking me in the eyes, hers very serious and round.

'I … I don't want you speaking like this. I don't like it,' I muttered, blinking and turning my head away.

'But it's the truth,' she insisted.

'It's *not* the truth, Riya,' I said, angry now – angry at her, angry at her cancer, angry at the world, angry at her mother for giving this to her. 'You're not going to die. *You're only sixteen*. People our age don't die.'

'But I *am* going to die. I have a terminal disease,' she said, not a trace of emotion in her voice. 'That's a fact.'

'Shut up!' I shouted. 'Shut up, Riya! Just shut up!' I scrambled to my feet, grabbing her wrists, surprising Riya and myself even more. 'You're not going to die! Just shut up!'

I felt her squirming in pain. I wanted to slap her, but before I could raise my arm, all those stupid tears came running down my eyes, down my nose, everywhere down my face.

She couldn't see me like this. So I got up and left, walking with my limp, faster than I knew I should. At the gate, I ran headlong into B.P., who stumbled and dropped his briefcase, its contents spilling everywhere. I didn't pause or apologize or help him pick anything up. I just limp-ran as fast as my scrawny legs could take me, past the teachers' colony, past the principal's house, through the girls' hockey field, in the direction of a safe haven, the library. I could feel the wind frosting my face, the blood singing in my ears and, for the first time in my life, I understood just why Riya loved running so much.

56

TO APOLOGIZE FOR my outburst, I surprised her at her house the next day, clutching a bunch of wild roses. I hadn't ever given her flowers before but I supposed vaguely that girls were supposed to like things like these.

'Are those from Principal Sir's garden?' she asked me, peering at my ragged blooms.

'Well…'

She broke into a laugh. 'You know how angry Principal Sir's wife will be if she finds out?'

I looked down at the pink roses, smelling of mud and grass, which had already started to wilt. I should have known that Riya wasn't a typical sort of a girl. Just a few years ago, in my fear, I would have gone back to re-plant the blooms but not any more. Now I simply grinned.

'I'm sorry,' I said. 'I didn't mean to shout at you earlier. I was just…'

She cut me off before I could finish.

'It's okay, Specs.'

This made me pause. I hadn't expected for her to give in to me so kindly, she usually gave me such a hard time.

'It is?' I said, surprised.

And then she looked embarrassed. 'I'm so tired of everyone treating me like this patient all the time. No one ever gets angry at me any more. I … I just want things to be normal.'

I took her hand. I couldn't help but laugh. 'Normal is one thing you're not.'

'No,' she reflected. 'Maybe not, but I want things to be like before.'

'Then come back to school, Mrinalini and co. are desperately missing you,' I joked.

She shrugged and moved her hand away.

'Specs, don't joke. I'm serious. I want you to treat me normally. And I want things to be the way they used to be.'

'Okay, I won't bring you chocolates any more.'

Now she threw the roses at me.

I picked the petals slowly off my blazer and then looked up at her. For the first time I saw fear brimming in her eyes and for the first time I did something that I had never done with her.

'Everything *is* normal, Riya,' I said, knowing that I was telling her a big fat lie.

57

IT RAINED ON my birthday – a cold, hard, grey rain which clattered against the windows and soaked everything. I felt as grim as the weather, my heart as cold as my soggy feet. It seemed like the worst punishment to have lived seventeen full years and to live god knows how many more if Riya were not there.

I did not care about my birthday. If anything, I tried to make sure no one knew about it. We had a tradition of birthday bumps at Residency School where boys would throw you in the air and catch you as you came down, as many times as you were years old. But they did not always catch you, and this process was often repeated far more times than it was technically supposed to be. People were occasionally injured quite badly. On his fifteenth birthday one surd was so badly abused that he got permanent vertigo.

The other, less violent Residency School birthday ritual consisted of planting a tree and tending it for the rest of the year. This was mandatory, but wildly unpopular. So while every student planted the tree no one tended it (our school did not exactly produce many nurturers), so in one barren corner of the campus, by the junior school playground, were rows of dead trees.

I personally enjoyed looking after my trees, and I had eleven healthy trees – pine, cedar and deodar – distributed all across campus of Residency School. I enjoyed the rituals of tree growing, and the oldest tree was now three times as tall as me. This year though was different. This year I didn't feel like planting a tree – I didn't feel like giving life when it was being taken away from me.

So my seventeenth birthday passed like any other day. The day went on as usual – classes, prefect duties and then my daily visit to Riya which always moored my day. When I reached her house at 5.00 p.m., the doctor was over, she had a thermometer in her mouth, and a blood pressure machine strapped around her arm, and she couldn't talk to me. She looked small and somewhat irritated; she submitted to these medical examinations with less than perfect grace. I watched for a while from the doorway; then I felt a tap on my arm.

It was Jeevan Singh. She had written me a note. Jeevan had not forgotten my birthday, and was grinning, widely revealing several missing teeth, holding an extra-sweet cold coffee which meant that after the sugar high I would get a headache. Ever since I had become a prefect, I had changed even in Jeevan Singh's eyes, and now he was trying to make up for all of his previous bullying.

I unfolded the note and read in Riya's ant-like handwriting that she wanted me to meet her after evening prep in the library.

The library?

I was a little confused. The Residency School library lay at the end of the campus, next to the waste processing plant, a mostly empty building, full of books, ancient computers and dust. I, of course, had spent a lot of time there but I could only say that for myself. I suspected that Riya had probably only been there a few times on mandatory visits. The library was not a place that anyone at Residency School went to out of choice.

I couldn't say no to her though I was angry at her. For what

I couldn't quite comprehend. Was it her fault that she was sick and with the doctor when I came? So after supervising prep, I slipped out of the side door and made my way across campus to the library, which, as I expected, was bolted and locked. I wondered why they even bothered to lock it up – who would possibly want to steal anything from here? But then again Residency School boys sometimes vandalized property for fun.

It was cold after the downpour and I shivered under my coat, listening to the screaming crickets that had replaced the birds. Footsteps broke into the night and Riya appeared, her eyes huge in her face now and her skin so pale that it shone.

'Specs?'

She stood there so thin, her clothes hanging on her.

I stepped forward. 'I'm here.'

'Happy birthday, Specs,' she shyly said.

'Thanks,' I murmured, my anger evaporating into the air.

'Let's go inside.'

'Inside? It's locked.'

'I have the key.'

'How?'

She winked at me and then fiddled with the lock. It took her a while to unbolt the big iron lock, but she did it finally, and we slipped in.

At night, the library was more monstrous and gloomy than in the day and now the smell of damp things filled the air.

'Why are we here?' I said in a whisper, out of habit, though there was clearly no one here.

'I guess because it's the library, and you love books.'

She produced a small torch, took my hand and led me to a corner. I followed her, our footsteps echoing in the dark. Then I saw on the table, a small black forest cake and two spoons.

I didn't know how to react – I wasn't used to gestures of this sort from anyone, let alone her. I turned to her.

'Do you like it?' she asked, looking at me intently in the torchlight.

I tried to speak, but I felt choked.

'Yes … yes, I do,' I croaked. 'That cake, it looks really good.'

'Let's try?' she asked and lit the candle on top of the cake. 'Make a wish, Specs.'

I closed my eyes and without thinking even for a second, I blew out the candle. I opened my eyes and caught her looking at me. We both knew what my birthday wish would be this year, and every other year. She had forgotten a knife and so I cut the cake with a spoon, and then before I put a piece into my mouth, I put a piece in hers.

'Delicious,' I said.

'I made it,' she said with a grin.

'You did not.'

Riya cooking? I couldn't imagine it. There was nothing, not in the least bit, domesticated about her.

'Okay fine,' she admitted. 'I didn't, but I watched while Jeevan did.'

She now pulled out a present wrapped in red paper from the pocket of her coat and handed it shyly to me. 'Your present.'

I could not remember the last time I had received a birthday present. Last year, she had wished me and given me a card, and that card had meant everything to me. I still had it, tucked inside my maths book because it brought me good luck.

Now I was at a loss of words.

'What … what is it?'

'Open it,' she urged gently.

I tried to spread the paper neatly so I could preserve it – preserve it like I tried to preserve everything at that time, every image, every memory, every keepsake, like the specimens in our biology lab suspended in formaldehyde, but patience was not one of Riya's virtues.

'Just open it, Specs.'

I tore it open and folded the pieces into my pocket – I would tape them back together – and then inspected my gift. It was a book: *The Man Who Knew Infinity: A Life of the Genius Ramanujan.* I turned it over and read the blurb.

'It's a good book,' she said quietly.

'It looks like it.'

'I read it … twice.'

'You did?'

Riya had never been one for reading. She had often asked me why I read so much and what I got out of it. I had never properly answered that question until finally one day when we were on the track, she running, me reading, and I had forgotten to time her because I was so absorbed in the book.

'What's in that book that you can't put it down?' she had asked, kicking sand all around.

I had thought about it for a second and then told her, 'It takes me to the same place that you go to when you run.'

She had never asked me that question again.

Now I felt the book, breathed the smell of the new pages, rubbed the sharp corners. And as I did so I looked at her, her face lit by the candle, framed in the tiny pulsing glow.

'I couldn't give you a book for your birthday that I hadn't even read.'

I was stunned. Buying a book was one thing, but reading it *twice*, for someone who struggled with reading more than five- or six-letter words? I knew how hard it must have been.

This gesture wasn't like her. Riya was not of this world; her mind never focused on mundane details like birthdays.

'Thank you,' I finally muttered, too embarrassed now to look up at her. When I did look up though, she smiled at me and pushed a strand of hair out of her face which was like an angel's in the light of the torch.

'You're a genius you know, Specs. Like him,' she said, pointing to the cover of the book.

'No, I'm not.'

'You are, Specs – never forget that.'

Then she gathered the remains of the cake, the box of candles and the spoons and though I could have stayed here all night, I knew that we had to leave.

Outside, the rain was falling again and in the inky darkness, we both stood there letting the raindrops run like tears down our cheeks, letting it soak our hair and spread like stains on our uniforms. Suddenly, the rain stopped, and the silver-white moon burst through the clouds. Then she took my damp hand in hers and pressed it once against her cheek.

58

ZUGZWANG IS DEFINED as a situation in chess where any move will result in an immediate and certain loss. Step one way, checkmate, step the other, checkmate. I was a master of this move, but little did I know that this move, *my* move, would be played so skilfully against me.

Even now, after all these years, I still remember him perfectly. Rajat Sinha. A tenth-standard boy who looked like a pretty girl. His skin was very pale and his eyes were topped by curled eyelashes so long that they seemed to touch his brows. I remember he had very red lips that turned purple in the cold.

Joining Residency School in the tenth standard was never an advisable move in the best of circumstances, and Rajat certainly did not present the best circumstances. Almost immediately, he became the butt of every joke and the centre of every prank. It was rumoured that they had found gay porn magazines underneath his mattress. He was a bully's dream – pale and skinny, reading expensive imported comicbooks that inevitably got snatched away, walking to prep alone, eating dinner with the juniors, being on the walk and run squad.

It wasn't often that the boys had such a perfect target. In some ways, he was more vulnerable than I had ever been: at least I had grown up at Residency School; at least I had my studies. I wondered why his parents had sent him here in the first place, because there wasn't a sporty bone in his body. But then, who was I to ask that question? I figured there were other guardians who had been as clueless as mine.

I knew Rajat had it hard. In a strange way, I felt close to him because I understood his humiliation, so I cut him as much slack as I could – not penalizing him for being late because someone had probably locked him in the dorm, not reprimanding him when he came to line-up wearing the wrong uniform because someone had probably thrown the right one away. I never reported him to Ansari Sir because I knew he would have beaten him, and Rajat already got beaten up every other day. Despite having been bullied in the worst way myself, I was shocked by the brutality and cruelty of the boys with whom I lived, with whom I had grown up. I never could have imagined that they would resort to such violence.

They found Rajat Sinha lying in a field next to Dhobi Ghat, three fractured ribs, a broken arm and a badly shattered thigh. He had lost close to a litre of blood from a wound in his head that they later found out had damaged his brain.

The school authorities never found out who did it, or what the reasons were. All anyone knew was that it happened in the middle of the night, and there was no visible clue to who the perpetrators were. That was the miserable irony of our boys – they would devour the weak in seconds, but they would also protect the pack. Residency School emphasized brotherhood and loyalty and being a sneak was the worst thing that a boy could ever be, except for maybe being gay, which appeared was possibly Rajat Sinha's crime.

Despite its gruesome violence, the incident may have slipped past unnoticed, as so many crimes at Residency School had in the past. But Rajat Sinha's father owned a local media channel, and the news of the attack spread like wildfire. Much to the horror of the school, the incident made the front page of local papers, and pictures of Rajat Sinha, his family, the principal, the board of governors, and even Ansari Sir were in the press every day for close to a week. Funnily enough, the episode had the strange consequence of causing the normally insular and apathetic students at Residency School to take a keen interest in the outside world, running to the library to get their hands on newspapers, tracking every bit of coverage.

The days that followed Rajat's attack were out of a movie – journalists lurked around in dark corners, the police swarmed in and out of the school, a team of cops set up base in our house to investigate the case. Under immense pressure to find the culprits, every single Ashok House boy was finger-printed and every single teacher too.

Our esteemed school even made national news as the 'Residency School scandal' broke and a big 'exposé' was run on the cloistered world of elite Indian boarding schools – the bullying, the beatings, the brutality. The reality was that this breaking 'news' was information any student learned in his first two weeks.

The school hadn't received this kind of bad press in many years. The board of our school was an illustrious one, consisting of many national luminaries, and we were known as one of the nation's finest and oldest schools. On the inside, we knew what the school was really like, but to the outside world, the impression was of bonhomie and building bonds for a lifetime. Now a boy had been almost beaten to death just because some boys were having fun. The board tried to cover it up, but when that failed, they resorted to the oldest Residency School ethos: blame and break the weak. The board was at the principal's throat, who in turn was at Ansari Sir's throat, who was so angry and frustrated that he beat up so many boys that his steel ruler finally snapped in two.

Within the house, chaos ensued but the guilty remained cloaked. Questions floated about in an atmosphere of tension and suspense. Would the culprits be found? Would Ansari Sir be kicked out? Would Principal Sir resign? Who would the new housemaster be?

Being prefect of Ashok House and technically in charge, I found myself in the centre of it all. I was taken to a small room where the police had set up headquarters and I was questioned for hours. I gave all the right answers to the questions asked of me. Who were his friends (all), who were his enemies (none), was bullying common in the house (no), and did the teachers beat the kids (never).

I went through all the motions and toed the school line, doing what a boy in my position had to do. But there were times when I saw Rajat's pictures in the papers, or when the boys whom I suspected were wolfishly lurking around, that I felt so wretched that I was almost ill. I asked myself again and again if there was anything that I could have done to save Rajat. Maybe, if all those months ago, I wasn't such a coward and I had reported Vikram and his gang? Maybe if I had snitched on the ones I suspected? Instead, I had deleted the shameful incident from my mind. I had shut my eyes to all signs of torture. I was in charge of a place where a boy had nearly died.

And with that, I fell permanently out of love with Residency School. It had never been my place but it had always been my home. With this one incident it was as though I'd slipped on a pair of spectacles after a long time of deliberate fuzziness and I was seeing clearly now the corrupt hell that my school had slowly become.

I was so absorbed in the frenzy – and Riya's gradually deteriorating condition – that I didn't even notice the signs of my own downfall. I didn't see the cold stares I got from the assistant housemaster, I didn't notice how the boys no longer paid heed to me and I didn't notice the number of boys who didn't show up when I took assembly. I didn't even notice that I sometimes walked into an empty classroom during prep.

Had I noticed something was amiss, I could have spoken to Ansari Sir or some of the other teachers who would have been on my side. I could have taken some precautionary political measures, made a paper trail, guarded my rear flank. But none of this struck me, and I remained clueless until it was much too late.

Vikram, on the other hand, was slowly and resolutely marshalling his forces. He was, unequivocally, back to being the golden boy. This, no matter how much of an ostrich I was, I could not have missed. No matter what his transgressions, he had a certain inborn charm that drew people to him and made them want to follow him. When the principal or the senior teachers came to the house, he was always around, taking charge, giving instructions, effectively solving problems, making others run around.

Even Ansari Sir, who I knew for a fact hated Vikram, seemed to be falling for his charm. As Ansari Sir walked around in a daze, fearful that he may lose his job, Vikram was at his sycophantic best. He was at Ansari's Sir's beck and call, running to get him a glass of water or the cane that he had left behind, carrying his notebooks for him and completing his unfinished tasks. He even joked around with him and jollied him, reassuring him that no one could have known about Rajat, insisting that the perpetrators would be caught and expelled quickly, assuring Ansari Sir that his rightful place as leading faculty at Residency School would soon be restored. It helped, of course, that Vikram had led Residency School to victory at the hockey nationals for the first time in ten years and that since he had been back he had won so many medals that I had simply lost count.

Steadily, Vikram rallied his troops against me, even as I remained utterly and absolutely oblivious. First, it was the boys, and then the house staff. Then even ancient Ansari Sir was brainwashed and was heard muttering about Vikram being a tower of strength in a trying time. Systematically, all my allies were replaced or removed, a pitiless pressing sweep. Vikram made sure that they all saw how inept I was, how I couldn't silence the boys or make them walk in line, how disorganized I was that things under my charge – the attendance register, exit slips, dorm records and even petty cash – were disappearing.

I didn't notice any of it, not because I was stupid, but mostly because I was living in some sort of hallucinogenic daze. I was hardly sleeping, surviving on less than three hours of sleep a night and studying well into the night because I had fallen desperately behind. And then I would read nonstop about cancer till the morning birds sang.

59

THE TRAP WAS finally sprung on a Friday night. I had visited Riya after supper, and half-heartedly studied for a chemistry test. Now I was staring out of my window, towards her house – which I found myself doing more and more.

Without warning, my door burst open. It was Ansari Sir who stormed into my tiny room and slapped me so hard that he knocked the glasses off my face.

'Sir…' I said, aghast.

'Where are the attendance registers?' Ansari Sir raged.

'Sir, I gave them to you…' I muttered, but he was in such a frenzy that he didn't hear a word.

Ansari Sir had gone purple in the face. 'Principal Sir has asked me three times. This *disgusting* behaviour can't go on. We *cannot* have prefects like this at Residency School,' he screamed, saliva dripping down his chin.

I was confused. I had placed the registers on his desk this morning. The police had asked for them, something to do with the case.

Ansari Sir continued pitilessly. 'You *don't* take prep, you're *late* for assembly. The teachers are complaining about your marks. If we had *proper* people in charge, people who could *control* these boys, none of this would have *ever happened*.'

'Sir…' I started, trying to explain myself, but when I saw the fury on his face, I stopped. He wouldn't listen, no matter what I said.

He drew himself up to his full height of just over five feet. He quivered, as though fighting to free himself from his tiny frame. 'You are a disgrace to the school. You should be *ashamed* of yourself,' he growled.

For an instant, he raised his arm, and I braced for another slap. But then he thought otherwise. He walked out of my room, slamming the door hard, my face burning from the slap and with shame.

60

THE NEXT MORNING, I was formally removed from my prefecture, and Ansari Sir took my badge away – actually, both mine and my co-prefects', though I suspected that it was really mine they were after. The ceremony was simple and desultory. Before Principal Sir, Ansari Sir and a few peons as audience – in the gloom of Ansari Sir's office – I unclipped the badge and placed it on the desk. Everyone, even the peons, glowered at us. And then it was done.

This, evidently, was the school's way of taking 'action' for what happened to Rajat Singh. Instead of investigating the crime or actually capturing the perpetrators, they decided to make an example of the prefects, the senior boys who were meant to lead the house but had instead taken it completely off track. It was our lack of control, which had led to the violence; we had failed to do our duties to the school.

Apparently, no prefect badge had ever been taken away mid-term in the history of Residency School. Extenuating circumstances called for extreme action, the school authorities said. It looked like I had made some sort of permanent dent in the school's reputation, as its biggest disgrace.

In an ironic turn of events, Vikram, the biggest and most vicious bully of them all, was given my badge. Ansari Sir suddenly turned, thumped his back and crowed with delight. He announced at assembly that Vikram was a natural leader, and would bring back discipline to the school.

It was then, seeing Vikram's smug grin, that the pieces fell together, and like the moment of clarity when you have arrived at the solution of a difficult integration in the simplest of ways, I grasped it all for what it really was: a set-up from start to finish.

Vikram's father, a hard-faced man with a beak nose and recently elected MLA, turned up in the papers vouching for the school. According to him, the 'scandal' was just the media playing up an incident that had never actually taken place. The Residency School was the best school in the country, with the highest ethical and pastoral standards. It was impossible this had really happened: it was faked, falsified and fictional. And just like that – because a powerful person said so – the pictures of Rajat in the press, with the Residency School tie tied like a noose around his neck, went away as quickly as they had appeared. It was as if none of it had ever happened: not Rajat's beating, not Vikram's expulsion, not my prefectship. And so I was once again just an obscure school boy, no immortalizing badge, nothing that made me different any more.

61

IT WAS JUST a badge, just a stupid, fake-gold badge. But yet, I felt like broken glass, shattered into a million little pieces that would never again rejoin. But I had to pick up the pieces and I had to move on. I couldn't let them get to me – Riya was the only one who deserved my tears. Yet, no matter what I told myself, I felt myself spiralling down. What would everyone think of me? What would they be talking about? How I was once so clever, so powerful, maybe even well-liked, but now how I was so pathetic and so dumb.

Riya helped me keep it in perspective. 'It's just a badge – a *pin* really,' she said to me.

'I know,' I said, holding my head in my hands, an empty feeling in my heart and a hole where the heavy badge had been pinned.

How could I explain what I was feeling when I didn't quite understand it myself? I knew that I had never really deserved this badge – it had been a wild stroke of luck. Or more than luck, it had been Riya, her luck, her faith. And now I wasn't just losing the badge. I was losing what I had accomplished because of her.

Riya tugged at my sleeve and then when I wouldn't look up, she pinched my ear, forcing me to look up at her.

'Tell me, Specs, what did he look like when he went up the stage to collect his badge?'

'Like a pig,' I grumbled, rubbing my stinging ear.

'And Ansari Sir?

'He just stood there, drool dripping down his chin.'

'And Vikram smiled like a greasy fool,' she said with a laugh. 'That rhymes, you know, your poetry is finally rubbing off on me. Is he still putting that shiny gel in his hair?'

'His hair shines almost as much as his badge,' I glumly said.

She laughed so loudly that she broke out into a terrifying cough. For several seconds, she held her mouth in her handkerchief.

I looked at her with concern, but then she looked up, eyes smiling bright.

'Riya, this isn't funny, you know.'

'But it is,' she said with a grin.

'Maybe to you,' I mumbled, sulking and staring at my shoes.

She threw her hanky at me, a crumpled pink thing which landed near my shoe. I picked it up and snuck it in my pocket.

'Come on, Specs! It's just a silly badge.'

'It's just, you know ... demeaning,' I said in an embarrassed voice.

'No, I don't know. I don't think anyone but you really cares.'

'You don't understand,' I said, taking off my glasses and rubbing my eyes. 'I even have to wear the same uniform as everyone else.'

Now she was laughing again. I was aware how silly I sounded: me, who owned only two shirts and a single pair of trousers, complaining about my clothes. But it still stung.

'It's not funny,' I complained.

'You never cared about all this stuff before – badges and uniforms. And now seeing you all torn up over this, it's just ... funny. Plus, it's winter now. Everyone wears the same sweaters, even *prefects*.'

When she saw that I hadn't cheered up, she tried again in a gentler tone. 'Look, take mine. I don't need them any more.'

She reached into a drawer and put four glimmering orbs in the palm of my hands. Riya had more badges than anyone else in school. She had been athletics captain and girls' sports captain for two years in a row. She had four badges when most people had one and very rarely two.

At Residency School, your badges were your identity, your most prized possessions, and looking at her badges lying like jewels in my palm, the depth of her compassion struck me like a hard slap. Here she was losing her life, yet trying to make me feel better about a ludicrous badge. And in that instant, I saw it all from her eyes. The pettiness, the drama, the politics. The change happened in a matter of seconds, my frown twisted into a smile and suddenly, unexpectedly, we started to laugh.

We laughed the kind of laugher that borders on hysteria, the kind that makes your tummy hurt and every time I would almost calm down, just looking at her would set me off again. I hadn't laughed like this in months and now I felt my problems floating away like helium balloons. That was the thing with her, she could make me laugh, even when I wanted to cry.

When we finally managed to stop, she asked me, still red in the face, 'Now that you're not a prefect any more, Specs, can I ask you for something?'

'Anything,' I said, gathering my breath.

'Will you take a trip with me?'

'A trip?' I gasped.

'I'm serious,' she said, though she didn't sound serious at all.

'I'll go wherever you want to go.'

'Okay, then apply for leave and finish all your schoolwork. We'll leave day after tomorrow.'

'All right,' I said, not giving it a second thought. 'Your wish is my command.'

I heard the final night bell toll. I didn't want to leave but it was time to go. I got up from the steps and walked back to my bike, looking at the badge that I had taken from her. It was her Athletic Captain badge from this year, the one that she had worn so close to her heart. I wouldn't wear it right now while I was at school, but I knew then and there that I would always keep it in my breast pocket where it would be even closer to my heart. And I always have.

62

TWILIGHT FALLS, STEEPING the mountains in shades of blue that spread upwards like a dye. The moon rises, touching each peak until the long horizon glitters against an electric-blue sky. In the distance immediately ahead of me, I see the faint outline of a particular mountain, a geometric cone, just like my little son would have drawn. It looks so perfect, so radiant that I wonder for a moment if any of it is real.

I swerve off my path, off the route that will lead me to the school. Instead, I go down a broken road in the direction of that perfect mountain, taking a journey that I had with her so many years ago.

By the time I reach my destination, the night is wrapped in rich velvety darkness, but the moon is so bright that I don't need to switch on my headlights. I have been driving for almost ten hours but I am not tired; instead, I am charged with a sort of a nervous energy.

My car bumps and jostles on the pitted road as I drive towards the settlement which looks eerie and mysterious at this hour, colourful prayer flags fluttering in the cool breeze. I stop at a cigarette stall where a group of people are huddled around a small crackling TV, sipping cups of steaming tea.

I want a cup of the salty-sweet butter tea, but I know it is getting late, and I don't have much time.

'The master?' I ask.

They nod and point to a dark road on the right.

I drive down the street guided only by the light of the moon and arrive outside a simple one-storey house, the only sounds, the crunching of the gravel underneath the tyres of my car.

The lights are on, but the little house seems deserted. I knock nervously on the door and within seconds, a red-faced young man wearing a maroon robe opens the door.

'Are you here to see the master?' he asks, without preamble.

'Yes,' I say, more to myself than to the young man. 'I'm here to see the master.'

I am ushered into a small lamp-lit room, where I wait for a few minutes. I am sitting on a bamboo rug that covers a dark wooden floor. It is cold and I shiver in my thin T-shirt. A few minutes later, the young man brings me a cup of steaming butter tea, which I gladly take. As I wait for it to cool, I wonder for the millionth time what I am doing here. I am on the verge of leaving when he finally returns and beckons me to follow.

The young man shepherds me into a little room and there he is, exactly as I remembered him – brown, wrinkled and round, with a smile that engulfs his face and small eyes which disappear when he laughs. My eyes stray for a moment to the photos on the walls, pictures of an old man with groups of people, and I realize that this laughing man sitting in front of me isn't the one I had seen all those years ago.

He catches my surprise and says with a sad smile, 'My master, he left his body last year.'

'Oh…' I sit down, taking a seat in the same room that I had sixteen long years ago. 'I'm sorry to hear that.'

I introduce myself and out of habit, I hand over my card. I tell him that I came to see his master many years ago with a close friend. It is strangely hard to talk; I suspect it is the incense choking my throat. 'Your master, he helped her … and me as well. I will always remember him.'

'My master was a great man, he was very, very wise.'

I can only clear my throat. He looks at me for a moment, then asks me gently, 'What can I do for you?'

I stare at him blankly, thinking that I didn't really know myself.

The spiritual calm that radiates from him is so potent that for a dizzying moment I am glad that I have come.

Finally I say, 'It's for my friend, the one with whom I came to see your master. I'm seeking blessings for her.'

He smiles widely, displaying his toothless gums. 'You, young man, have a habit of worrying, don't you?' he says in a scolding tone. 'I can see in your eyes that you are very worried. But there is nothing for you to worry about. She is safe, your friend, and she is home. The soul is very wise, wiser than you or me. When it leaves, it knows exactly how to find its way back.'

Seeing that I am still tense, he laughs and places a hand on my shoulders. 'Your friend, she is travelling in infinity, as free as a speck of light.'

I have heard what I need to hear, and so I thank him and leave. I find my car and begin driving in the darkness, making my way up the mountain, now for the final stretch.

63

WE LEFT ON our journey at the crack of dawn. I hadn't slept much, nervous and excited about the journey ahead. I was also somewhat anxious. I had avoided B.P. since my badge had been taken away, and now I would have to spend hours with him enclosed in a small car. B.P. had rooted for me to become prefect and the thought that I had embarrassed him made me want to sneak into a dark hole and never come out.

At first the silence in the car was discomfiting for me. It was clear right away that B.P. didn't want to talk – the only way he had acknowledged me was by giving a stiff polite smile and signing my exit pass. A driver was driving, B.P. was in the front seat and Riya and I were at the back. I was wearing my only set of civilian clothes – a pair of jeans, a T-shirt and a coarse maroon sweater my grandmother had once sent. Riya wore her usual navy tracksuit with a light grey woollen hat that made her look like a little girl.

The mood eased as B.P. nodded off to sleep and gently snored in the front seat. Riya and I whispered to each other and passed each other notes.

Soon Riya too fell asleep, her cap covering her eyes, headphones wrapped around her head. I had given her the Walkman to use for her running but she never used it for that. I stayed awake for some time, thoughts racing through my mind. I wondered where we were going. What were we doing? Riya had been very vague about everything, more so than usual, not saying much about the trip.

Eventually, lulled by B.P.'s snores, I too closed my eyes. I didn't even notice falling asleep – that's how tired I was – exhausted from school politics, drained by my many losses, I do not even remember if I had dreamed.

We arrived three hours later just as I awoke. We were in a valley, surrounded by steel-coloured mountains poised against a lavender sky. The peaks here seemed to be closer and more majestic, with a gleam different from the mountains that surrounded Residency School. The sun here was brighter too, and I shielded my eyes as I got out of the car.

We were outside a small, indistinct guesthouse two storeys high made of grey cement. Someone came out to get our bags. Riya and I stretched our legs and hung out by the car while B.P. checked us in. B.P., who hadn't said more than two words to me, handed me a set of keys. Riya and he were sharing a room while I was to have my own. I could tell that despite the fatigue in her eyes, Riya was excited. B.P., I could see by the constant frown on his face, was worried. As for me, as usual I wasn't sure how to feel.

As I waited in my room, wondering what to do with myself, Riya knocked on my door. She had changed into a pair of jeans and a fitted cream sweater that I had never seen her wear before. Her hair – usually tied up in a ponytail – was now loose, and it lay in messy curls covering her shoulders, neck and back. Her face was pale and her cheeks were flushed, matching the colour of her lips.

'That's a nice sweater,' I blurted out, reeling under her extraordinary effect. She looked so beautiful sometimes that it physically hurt.

'It was Ma's,' she said simply, pinching her sweater with her fingers, and then looking out of the window to the mountains hidden by the clouds.

I knew that there was something on her mind. She paced and fidgeted and twitched the curtains back and forth. 'Do you think all this is really strange?'

I was confused. 'What's strange?'

She studied the floor before she looked up at me. 'All this, us being here.'

'No, not really,' I lied.

Truth be told, all I could think was what in the world was I doing here. All Riya had told me was that we were going to see someone important, but she had not divulged any further details. And I had not asked.

'My mother came here, you know,' she said, looking up at me now.

'She did?'

'Right before she died.'

'Why?'

'To visit the master we're going to see.'

'Oh,' I said, confused.

'Papa says that he helped her out.'

'The master?'

'Yes.'

'Is that why we are here?' I asked, still quite confused.

She shrugged and puckered her lips. 'I guess so. I came here too, you know, with her before she died. I don't remember much, I just have vague memories of this nice time. Thank you,' she said, embarrassed and now looking at her feet.

'For what?'

'For coming with me.'

Her face was thoughtful, she looked at me intently, as if she was going to say something else, but then we heard B.P. calling for her in the hallway.

'I better go,' she said, leaving me, as always, a little dazed as she walked swiftly out of my room.

64

WE SAT IN front of a wizened man with a wrinkled face, broad smile and only a few teeth. The room was warm and bright with sunlight streaming in from the large windows, creating sharp patterns on the floor. B.P. sat with us for a little while, but soon quietly slipped out of the room.

The master looked at Riya, nodding happily. He was totally bald, with long feathery, snow-white eyebrows that looked like doves ready to take flight. He took her hands into his and held them tight. Riya looked up at him. I wonder what was going on in her head, but I didn't have to wait long for an answer.

With hesitation in her voice, she finally blurted out, 'They say I'm dying. That I have thirty days to live.'

He looked at her, blinking his old eyes, and then much to my surprise he laughed out loud.

'I am dying too,' he said in a calm and matter-of-fact way. 'Your father and your friends too. We all die, little by little. Just a matter of time, isn't it? Your time is just a little sooner than mine.'

The way he said it, death didn't sound very sad at all. He bobbed his head and continued with laughter in his voice. 'Death is not as scary as it sounds. Death is just a stage of life. Being a baby, that's one stage, a teenager another; being an old man like me, that is a stage too. Death is like that, a stage of life we have to pass through. The only reason we get scared is because we don't know what it is like and we don't know where we will go.'

He chuckled again and tugged at the maroon robe draped around his neck.

'Don't be scared. You are a brave girl, and death, like life, is better if we just accept what is coming our way. Why not accept and celebrate death just like we accept and celebrate life? Death is a wonderful way to find life. Why be scared? It's the one thing that will happen to all of us without fail. It's the only thing we can predict. About anything at all.'

'But I want to run more races – what about that?' she asked him softly, studying the sunlight on the floor for a moment and then looking up at him with a sort of longing in her eyes.

He paused and then with a wise, quiet look, said, 'You will, you will. All of your wishes will come true, that is the nature of this soul. God is a very good timekeeper, and for every one of us the clock works differently. For each one of us, there is a time to love and a time to die. But, at this moment, you have to accept what is coming your way. And acceptance means letting go of the things you are attached to. You don't have to do it all at once. Do it slowly. One by one, like the petals leave the rose.'

The master seemed very satisfied. He sat back and almost seemed to be laughing except that he was silent. He was a strange, silly, happy man, but in some way he also seemed to be the most powerful person I had ever met.

Then he said, shaking his bald head from side to side, 'Don't fear death. Trust that only wonderful things are ahead. These days, they put people on painful medicines, hoping and hoping, wanting more days, but that makes things worse. We all have our time, every one of us, and there will be more time for many more souls.'

He crinkled his nose and peered into her eyes.

'Here, we celebrate the day the person dies like the day a person is born. If people didn't cry at funerals, they may be a lot of fun.'

The master now burst into laughter, very pleased at his own joke. At this, Riya smiled and so did I.

'Can I ask you something?' she said in a lighter voice.

'You can surely ask.'

'Is there such a thing as God?'

This time, he smiled so deeply his eyes disappeared into his leathery face. 'That you exist is proof that there is God, because if God didn't exist, how could we? All these scientists, they try to explain the origin of life, but after all these years and centuries of research they have only come so far,' he said, holding his fingers an inch apart.

She thought about this for a moment, chewing on her lip.

'That something that you feel, that little spark inside? That something is the only thing that lasts through this life, through this death, through the next life, the next death and all other lives and deaths that will come your way. That something is the God within you, that God which you are questioning right now.'

His eyes were very bright now and Riya looked up at him with so many questions in her eyes.

'You ask a lot of questions, young lady, but remember this for the rest of your days because it will give you peace. Nothing is permanent and nothing will last. Everything, everyone will die, just at different times. Life is a sequence of births and deaths and for new experiences to happen, old ones need to die.'

The master now suddenly exclaimed, 'I remember your mother now! She, like you, asked many questions.'

'She did?'

'She did. I told her that all the answers already lay within her, she just had to look inside. You, my young friend, can do the same.'

A wistful look came over him. It seemed strange to have such a happy man look even remotely sad. 'She came here with a small baby.'

'That was me,' Riya said.

The master was so delighted by this that he laughed and clapped his hands.

'Oh yes! Your mother, she was very strong. She was not scared of death, not like most people. She was prepared for death, you know.'

'She was?'

'Yes, yes she was.'

And then he looked at me, sitting in a corner.

'And who is this, this young man?'

'He's my best friend,' Riya said simply.

He beckoned me. My leg had fallen asleep and I dragged myself to the cushion, closer to them both.

'What's your name, young friend?' he asked.

'Nikhil.'

'*Nikhil.* A good name for a good boy. A fine boy. You, my young friend, you have a role to play too. You are an important part of Riya's life and you will be an important part of her death.'

I looked wide-eyed at him. I had no desire to be part of anyone's death, let alone Riya's.

'Don't worry, friend!' he said, looking at Riya, and then back at me.

He took my hand in his and I am amazed by how warm and welcomed I now felt. He came closer to me and whispered in my ear.

'I will tell you only good things. Now let me share a little secret with you…'

65

UNTIL NOW, I knew that she was dying, but I had not thought about death. I had understood death as something entirely separate from life. Now, however, it was dawning upon me that death exists not as the opposite of but very much a part of life. I knew that death could take you in an instant, squeezed out of a body during a car crash, but what I had never thought about was how death itself lived in life, embedded in each shiny cell. I had studied that amino acids changed into cells that gave us life but now I knew that the cells which kept you alive could kill you as easily too.

This visit to the master had given me a chance to see things in a way that I had not before. I had been in denial and now slowly that was starting to fade.

Right from the start, right from the time she had given me the news, Riya had seemed to know with chilling calm that she was going to die. I remember what the master had said to her right before we had left the room: 'You have thirty days left. Many people, most people, don't even have that. Live each day to the fullest and in the best possible way.'

Riya was resilient, the kind of fighter that I could never be. She was not giving up on life, she was in fact doing something much more difficult. She was accepting this *without* a fight, and this wasn't easy for her, who had been born to fight and to win. I realized then something that she had already discovered – life wasn't a race. These are the words I had myself said to her. Life wasn't meant to be fought or won, life was meant to be lived, and Riya, by not fighting with death, *was* living every day of her life.

66

AFTER WE LEFT the master's house, I felt as light as a dream. We wandered around the market, past the crowded noodle stands, red-cheeked women hawking us their wares, their pink-faced babies strapped to their back, the chiming sounds of the prayer wheels in the distance, the mountain sun on our back. I spent all my pocket money buying her a new tape for the Walkman that she now carried everywhere. We ate Maggi, gulping it down with soft drinks, and looked shyly into each other's eyes. I stole a few moments to hold her hand, until someone who looked vaguely like B.P. approached us from a distance. We quickly broke away, and then laughed when we realized that it was not him.

Here, in this magical town ringed with endless mountains, the sky was crystal clear. In the fading light of the afternoon, my worries also seemed to fade away and I felt that I was floating, a stray mountain cloud in the sky.

For a second I stopped as she walked ahead of me. She ran her hands through her messy hair and bent down to look at a book as the sun lit her face. She swivelled her head and caught me staring. This time, I did not look away. For that moment, everything felt exactly as it must, and if I could pause life for a moment and then return to it before the end, this was the moment that I would choose. There was no real profundity, no complexity, but in its simplicity it was bliss and it stands apart as the time that I was most happy and content.

We walked back to the guesthouse at the speed of snails, biding time before inevitably seeing B.P., but he was nowhere to be seen. I have worried throughout this trip about whether B.P. was watching me, watching us – but now I didn't care any more.

We went back to my small room. She switched on the TV, lying down on the bed. She was tired, and as she watched a silly show on TV, I watched her from the corner of my eye. I took in the upward slant of her mouth when she smiled, the downward when she sighed, her eyebrows arching above her eyes, the eyelashes fluttering up and down. I watched her as she fell asleep, and I moved closer to her, stroking her hair, touching her cool face with my fingers as she moved a little in her sleep. She was so close to me that her breath mingled with my own and then I closed my eyes and went off into her dream with her.

67

AS WE DROVE back the next day, B.P. looked tired, and he talked even less than usual, merely staring out of the window, a frown furrowing his face. Despite his dark mood, I was more relaxed. Riya seemed relaxed as well as she listened to her new tape while I read *Love in the Time of Cholera* by Gabriel Garcia Marquez.

After the first hour and a tea stop, B.P. seemed better and I noticed that he had a book of poems in his hand. He chatted with the driver about the latest cricket scores, and I felt a small pang, wishing that I too knew about cricket and could maybe play too. Perhaps then I would have something to talk about with B.P.

Another hour or two passed and I dozed off at the back of the car, waking suddenly to the wail of a passing truck. I rubbed my eyes and put my glasses back in place. B.P. was snoring softly now and Riya too was asleep. I scribbled a note for her and nudged her shoulder gently, trying to wake her up, but she didn't budge. I squeezed her hand but she didn't respond; her head just bobbed to and fro.

'Hey,' I whispered.

I said it loudly now, shaking her shoulder hard, touching her face. 'Riya? Riya? Are you sleeping?'

B.P., in the front seat, was slowly rousing.

'Riya' I said, loud and clear.

B.P. looked back with sleepy eyes; then he saw the fear in my eyes. He immediately took Riya by the shoulders and shook her hard.

'Riya,' he called.

But she just lay there.

He told the driver to stop the car and rushed to the back, immediately checking her pulse and splashing water in her face.

'Nikhil.'

'Yes, sir,' I said, worried out of my wits and also afraid that I would cry.

'Please go sit in the front.' And to the driver, B.P. said in an urgent hiss, 'Drive to the nearest hospital – very, very fast.'

68

THINGS WERE HAPPENING quickly, too quickly for me to understand – nurses, doctors, blue uniforms, white coats. The neon lights of the hospital buzzed and spat, the doors opened and closed with a pneumatic hiss. I stood by her side the whole time, in the centre of the emergency room, feeling a loud, horrible erratic thumping in my chest as if a dying animal was trapped inside.

'Wake up, Riya, wake up,' I whispered over and over again like a parrot gone cuckoo. She was mumbling now, her eyes opening, not looking at anything in particular and then closing again. B.P. was white with anxiety, his eyes aghast, but he was very calm. He spoke very slowly to me, to her, to the doctors, to everyone. He was an athlete, after all. If anyone was used to pressure, it was him.

At length, a team of young doctors took her away to a small room, wheeling her through the corridors. Someone asked me to wait outside, I don't remember who, but I stood there stupidly, my glasses slipping off my face, staring at them taking her away. I wondered if this could even be true; it seemed like just a moment ago we had been in the market, laughing and eating noodles.

Riya could not die. It was impossible for her to die, not when I needed her as much as I did. Not yet. I wasn't ready yet. I wasn't prepared to let her go. I needed more time. I couldn't let her die. What would happen to me once she was gone? Desperate thoughts rattled my brain and I felt like I couldn't move. Eventually, I dragged myself to a plastic chair and sat down, feeling utterly helpless – there was nothing, absolutely nothing that I could do but sit there, frozen with misery, staring dumbly at the stained hospital walls.

My body sank and I listened to my breath go in and out. I wondered if this was finally and really goodbye. No, it simply could not be. In my darkest moments, I had imagined how it would happen, but never once had it been like this. Patients sat around me, absorbed in their own pain, not caring about me or about her. I found myself oddly thinking of God, though I hadn't been one to pray for most of my life.

I eventually got up and walked, as if in a trance, to the small room where she was being kept for observation. She lay under a blue blanket and B.P. was sitting next to her on a chair, very still. I desperately wanted to go inside, but looking at both of them, I knew it was incorrect to intrude, so I went back to my chair.

Hours spilled past and I sat still, unable to sleep or eat or even read. Gradually, a creeping terror rose from a place beyond thoughts. It was like the chime of the Residency School bell, over and over, twelve times: 'Why her? Why her? Why not me? Can't I trade my life for hers?'

The reappearance of B.P. jolted me out of my thoughts. 'Have you eaten?' he asked.

'No, sir,' I said in a daze.

'I'll go get some food. You can go,' he said, pointing to her room and then walking away.

I tiptoed inside, nervous about what I would find. She was asleep now, a tube in her arm, the flashing red numbers on the machines, but I knew nothing about what they meant. So much for full marks in biology.

'Riya, please look at me,' I whispered and begged, squeezing my eyes shut, bending towards her. I wasn't prepared for her to die – not yet, not right now. *Please, please, please – not right now.*

'I'm looking, Specs,' she said in a drowsy voice, though her eyes were shut.

'You're awake?' I said, jerking back, my eyes opening wide and clear.

'Uh huh,' she replied.

'Are you okay?'

'It just hurts a bit.'

She opened her eyes, and, for a second, squinted blearily at me. One hand was on her side, and the other hand was splayed out, an IV stuck in her right arm. I don't know what part of her body was hurting, but I didn't want to guess. In that gown, I could see bruises up and down both of her arms.

'Is everything all right?'

'Will everyone stop asking me that? I'm sleepy, that's all,' she murmured. Even now she acted like nothing was wrong. She closed her eyes and dozed off into a drug-induced sleep.

I was startled by squeaky footsteps on the linoleum floor, and I saw that it was the doctor, a tired young man with a dirty white coat. A spider of anxiety crawled up the back of my neck and I quickly stood up, bracing myself for bad news.

'You're her brother?' he asked.

'No, a friend.'

'She'll be all right,' he said in a distracted way, scribbling notes on a pad. Somehow, I didn't trust what he said.

'Should I wake her?' I asked anxiously.

'No,' said the doctor, waving his hand in the arm, 'let her sleep.'

'What happened?'

'Low blood pressure, high altitude. She fainted, that's all,' he said brusquely.

After a brief, charged pause he looked up from his pad to say, 'But in her condition, it could be dangerous. She needs to rest.'

He then said definitively, 'Take her home and don't take any more trips.'

Then he left the room and handed me a piece of paper attached to which was a pink discharge slip. The lights in the room buzzed and winked and I was so relieved that I thought now I would be the one to faint.

Part 4

69

I TURN THE bend and there it is, exactly as I had left it all those years ago. The light is pale gold and dimming, but I can see the top of the Residency School dome, changing colours like a sunrise, first grey, then silver and then pink as I approach the entrance, which, after all this time, is still imposing.

'Alum,' I say to the liveried guards. They salute me and let me through, and I am suddenly in another world – a world of verdant hedges and acres of manicured lawn, of lush playing fields and red brick buildings, of gables and turrets and playing fields for as far as the eye can see. The buildings still glisten, though they are almost a hundred years old and I cannot help but notice that the marble clock tower, the heart of the school, now as back then, does not accurately keep the time.

Everywhere there are small bodies, their screams flying like cricket balls. The workers are trimming the lawns, sweeping the leaves that swirl like confetti and then litter the ground. I drive straight to Scindia Pavilion, drive past the main building, past the academic block and the boys' cricket field, and there it is looming in the distance, its stone walls seem to call out my name.

'Specs!' she calls, running towards me. Her face is flushed, her shorts bunched at her thighs, her legs thin and strong and brown. It's a midsummer evening and the air is unnaturally warm. She

is covered in a layer of sweat and she throws herself down on the grass, closing her eyes, her chest moving up and down.

Looking at her lying there on the ground, I want her so badly that I cannot look away. I am relieved that her eyes are shut because I cannot prise mine away. Suddenly her eyes flutter open and she catches me. Her mouth forms an 'O' of surprise. Embarrassed, I turn my head away.

She laughs her childish laughter.

'Oh, Specs,' she says, still catching her breath.

I don't know what to say.

'Come,' she says, patting the grass, 'come look at the sky with me.'

I lie down on my back next to her and look heavenward. The sun is slowly setting and we lie under the fading light, watching the slow hypnotic descent of the sun. Then, in a rare act of courage, I reach out and place my hand upon hers.

I feel her touch on my shoulder. I look up startled, her face is flushed. She brings her finger to my lips and I lie very still, holding my breath, nervously waiting, my heart swelling and swelling and swelling. Then I take a breath, opening my mouth to speak, and she suddenly leans forward and her lips touch my own. And just like that, under the setting sun and crimson skies, as the wind blows red sand into our faces, I kiss her lips, salty after her run.

It is a physical pleasure so intense that I know no other moment will ever compare to it. I feel foolish now for having been so afraid, for having waited so long, for having rehearsed the moment so carefully in my mind. Now, as I kiss her, it is the simplest thing in the world. My fear melts away like wax from a candle and all I can feel is warmth.

I walk into the small back room of the pavilion and it is exactly as I remember it; like so much of Residency School, it is as if time hasn't touched this place. There is dust and athletic equipment everywhere – rusty discuses thrown carelessly on the floor, a set of hurdles bent into a painful V and piles of worn-out spikes. I study the athletic records carefully on the wall, checking for her name. All her records have been broken – except one. The 400 metres, I knew, would stand, till the end of time.

Horror and dismay engulf me when I see that the stone walls have been painted freshly white. But then I move closer and touch the wall. I am almost absurdly relieved to discover they are still there, the names, behind the row of javelins, like they have been for sixteen years. I run my fingers over grooves and I trace our names chiselled deep into the wall.

She takes me there, into a small room in the pavilion. 'Athletics headquarters,' she says proudly.

'Impressive,' I reply, looking at the dark, dank room, a storage room of dusty equipment lined with rough wooden honour boards that contain all the school's athletic records. She points hers out to me – 100 metres, 200 metres, 400 metres, 800 metres, 1200 metres. All five belonged to her: as if I didn't know, I knew all her records, her timings – down to the second by heart.

'Now see this,' she says in an excited whisper, nodding to the old walls made of blocks of grey-black stone.

At first it isn't apparent, but when I look closely, I see hundreds of initials, names, hearts and years written on the wall. It is a powerful sight, proof of the same ancient urge that made people scratch cave paintings, carve statues, build tombs like the Taj Mahal: the need of all lovers everywhere to leave evidence of themselves, so something will remain when they are gone.

'What's this place? A vault of love?'

'Something like that.' She grins. 'It's a secret place.'

I trace the initials and florets and curlicues.

'Who knew this much love happened at this school?'

'But it does,' she says, staring at me solemnly. 'It happens everywhere.'

I use my pen to write our names on the wall, next to a pair of lovers' initials, 'IT ♥ TF – 1984'. I wonder briefly where they were today and what had happened to them.

'Not like that, Specs.'

'Then how?'

She is holding her spikes in her arms. She takes one shoe and with her fingers plucks out a metal pin from the sole.

She crouches, and, using the pin, etches our names into the wall. When she is done, she turns to me. I see that the tips of her fingers are covered in blood.

Her voice is satisfied. 'See, Specs, now it's forever.'

So there it is – 'Nikhil & Riya' forever engraved in the very veins of this school. She rocks back on her heels, stares at the wall for a second, admiring her handiwork, and then reaches out and touches our names, staining them red with her blood.

70

OUR SCHOOL WAS so small and insular that the Rajat Sinha incident had gripped everyone in its maddening vice. But now the scandal was old news and Riya had been gone an inordinately long time, the rumour mills begun to spin.

Someone said she was in Delhi preparing for the nationals. Others said that they had seen her on campus, driving out in B.P.'s car. Mrinalini claimed to know that she was in the mountains, undertaking altitude training for the Olympics. I was puzzled and a little bit amused by many of these accounts. When people asked me where she was, I was deliberately vague with my answers.

I sat at my desk trying to complete vast amounts of unfinished schoolwork. Vikram, holding a hockey stick in his hand, came into the bare room that should have been his. In a rare act of sympathy, Ansari Sir had not given away my room along with my badge. I never knew what induced his pity, though I suspected it may have dawned upon him about how useful I had been during the Rajat Sinha incident – and not only as a scapegoat. While Ansari Sir had spent weeks spinning off into his geriatric deliriums, I had hand-copied hundreds of pages of records, made long tedious reports and filled out extensive police paperwork.

Vikram looked around the room, studying the walls and piles of books.

I wondered vaguely if he were here to sneer at me, or lord over his prefecture. I hadn't seen him much since his investiture. None of it mattered to me though, not like the way it did before. I was too focused on Riya, everything else seemed immaterial.

'So where is she?' he asked casually, juggling the hockey stick in his hands.

I looked up at him, feeling no fear at all. 'Who?'

'Your little bird.'

'She's fine,' I muttered, pretending to be studying something in my book.

'I didn't ask how she was. I asked where she was.'

There was no way for me to escape this question. I was, after all, trapped in the confines of my room; his unerring sportsman's instinct for space and movement effectively blocked the only escape. I looked up at him and for a fleeting instant, I swear that I saw concern in his beady eyes.

At that moment, I heard the wheezy voice of Ansari Sir from the corridor. 'Vikram, my office please.'

Vikram, surprised at Ansari Sir's arrival, stepped away. To my surprise, he nodded stiffly at me. Ansari Sir popped into the doorway and peered at me, a curious look in his old eyes. Then he turned, closing the door behind him so quietly that even a small baby would not wake.

71

JUST ABOUT NOW, things began moving very quickly. For a few weeks, time had seemed to stand still, as if it was creating memories especially for me. Now it sped like a train that had a destination but was making very quick stops.

She too was changing fast. One moment, she was strong; the next, she was a sick girl staring at me with blank, listless eyes. She was thinner than I had ever seen her and was tired a lot, sometimes never even getting out of bed. Though these changes had been happening right in front of my eyes, I never quite registered them – like the slow deterioration of a tree, the stages so gradual they cannot be distinguished separately. But now, every time I looked at her, I saw a different Riya from the one I knew, the Riya I had first laid eyes on all those years ago in the tenth-standard classroom, the girl with the short skirt and the wild hair that matched her eyes, the girl who ran like a dancer on the tracks.

What upset me most – oddly enough – was when she stopped eating the food she had once gobbled like a starving teenage boy. I'd always teased her about being constantly hungry, about being able to eat far more than I could.

I spent the last of the money I had won in the GK competition on her favourite foods – chocolate bars, cream biscuits, imported caramel toffees, masala chips, but she hardly ate anything. She would thank me sweetly and tell me that she was saving the treat for later. The next day I would find everything still there by the side of her bed, little insects and bugs swarming around her food.

As she melted from body to bones, I knew somewhere deep within that I would be better off if I accepted it all. Earlier, my despair about her disease had been poisoned by hope. But now I was finally understanding that hope is a dangerous thing – it smoulders on and consumes you, bit by bit. Now my hope was lifting and the despair too was becoming lighter, like smoke drifting into the air.

I began wondering, was death really so terrible a thing? I wasn't sure any more. My parents had died, Riya's mom had died, and I would die one day too. What the master said was true. We all had to die at some point, and I wondered, was sooner really worse than later? Who knew? Maybe death would be a journey into another place, a place that was in fact magnificent, beautiful, a place where she and I could never be separated again. It struck me that maybe me wanting Riya to stay alive was simply my selfish desire of always wanting to be with her.

During this time, I found it helpful to heed the master's advice and to live in the present, mostly because thinking about the past was too painful, and thinking about the future was too grim. The present, it seemed, was really the best place for me, and so this is where I stayed, just Riya and me.

72

I DON'T QUITE remember whose idea it was. It could have been Riya's or B.P.'s; it might even have been mine. I talked a lot those days, trying to keep Riya's spirits high. Over time, the idea became a topic of discussion, then a hypothetical situation. At some point it became a plan: a get-together to break the news about Riya's condition to the batch.

At that time – mid-November – I was more or less living at Riya's house. Jeevan Singh expected me five minutes after the school day ended, and always had tea waiting. B.P. had withdrawn into himself and hardly ever spoke more than necessary words. However, following the trip to the master, he seemed to accept my constant presence, and would occasionally grunt in my direction. I counted this as tacit permission to keep visiting; though we both knew he wouldn't be able to keep me away.

We sat around her living room and debated the issue endlessly. She usually reclined on the sofa, covered with a blanket. I lounged on the floor by her side.

'Do you think it's a bit much?' she asked.

'It'll give you a chance to see everyone. They've been asking about you.'

'They have?'

'People *have* noticed that you've been gone.'

'Well, I don't care, and I don't want to see most of these people anyway,' she said with a shrug.

'You're going to have to at some point.'

'Why?'

'It's probably the right thing to do,' I said, now doubtful of the argument I was trying to make.

'There's nothing right or wrong about it,' she said firmly. 'It's my life. And death.'

In the end she was convinced by B.P. that a small gathering was appropriate though by now I had doubts about the wisdom of the plan. It would tire her and potentially distress her to see their reactions and deal with their questions. The more I thought about it, the less I wanted her to do this, but I also didn't want to say anything because I was painfully aware now that this could just be me being selfish, wanting her all to myself.

I told myself that it wasn't a big deal – just our batchmates on B.P.'s lawn, drinking juice and eating chips. We did that every day during tea, didn't we? But something about this whole affair bothered me. It felt like one of those 'farewell' teas that the school had for the staff when they were about to leave the school.

'What are you going to wear?' she asked me hesitantly, breaking my thoughts.

'Huh?'

'To the tea.'

'School uniform, I guess?'

'It's on Sunday.'

'Well, then something else.'

I only had one set of civilian clothes, so choice wasn't a problem for me.

'I don't know what to wear,' she said, chewing on her lip, playing with the sandwich that lay in front of her. Jeevan, I noticed, always put a plate of food in front of her, hoping, like me, that she would eat.

In the bare living room, the sun was streaming onto a part of her face. I suddenly realized how thin she was, how sick she really looked.

'Jeans maybe,' I said, swallowing hard, looking away, hoping that she hadn't noticed my expression. 'You've got those nice dark jeans.'

'They don't fit any more,' she said plainly.

'Maybe you should eat that then,' I joked weakly, pointing to the sandwich, avoiding looking at her tiny waist.

She flipped her hair. 'I'm not hungry.'

'You never are.'

She just rolled her eyes, clearly something else on her mind. I waited for her to continue, but she sat chewing the end of a straw. I couldn't tell what she was thinking. It had never been easy in the past and nowadays it was near impossible. I looked at her struggling with her thoughts, something so familiar to me that I almost laughed. How many times had I seen her like this, chewing on the end of a pencil struggling with an easy sum?

'I'll have to get something new,' she finally said.

I grew even more confused. I had never known Riya to express the slightest interest in typically girlish pursuits like shopping or fashion. Occasionally, she got excited about buying a pair of new spikes.

And then a thought struck me like lightning. Even though, to me, Riya was above this world, as bewitching and beautiful as any girl who had ever lived, the truth was that she was just a girl – a lovely girl who liked to run and eat chocolates, a girl who couldn't do mathematics to save her skin. Even though she seemed so strong and capable, she was human and she had human anxieties. She was concerned about the way she looked, and that I supposed was naturally how any girl would feel.

The following day, I bunked school to go shopping with Riya. Who could have ever imagined that, but then again bunking school for me these days had become more or less a norm. Luckily for me, as a crumb of glory from my prefect days, the gatekeepers didn't usually ask me for the exit pass. We went to the only option open to us, the town's only department store, if it even warranted such a title – a small two-floor building in the centre of a crowded marketplace. I could tell Riya was in a good mood by the way she chattered nonstop but even before she stepped into the store, she was so physically tired that she could barely climb up the stairs. The chaos and the crowds almost immediately overwhelmed her, but she insisted that we press on.

Part of me wished B.P. were here, as backup in case something happened. But I was desperate to buy her something that she would wear. We walked around the women's section – party dresses, blue jeans, T-shirts in bright colours, salwar kameez embroidered with gold and silver. She walked past everything, sometimes touching a thing to two.

Even just looking at things seemed to wear her down more and more.

I suggested that we could start at shoes. 'Shoes are easy,' I said, 'I can help you with those.'

'What do you know about shoes?' she joked tiredly.

So we went to the shoes section and she didn't protest when I bent down to untie her laces and take off her sneakers which, for a change, had no mud or grass stains. I told the salesman to get her size and then, for each shoe that he brought, I slipped them gently onto her feet, which seemed smaller and bonier than in the past.

It was a deeply odd feeling. Ever since I had known her, she had been stronger and faster than me. She would always slow down to walk by my side, and I had always yearned to be faster, stronger, so that she didn't have to always wait for me as I struggled to catch up.

Now, as I helped her walk upstairs because she couldn't do it herself, tied her shoelaces because she didn't have the strength to bend down, I realized that I had always dreamt that one day I would be her strength. But today, I would have given anything to go back, for her to be stronger than me, like she had been in the past.

When I caught her looking at me in an embarrassed way, I encouraged her the way I used to do with the sums that she couldn't do. 'It's part of the process,' I said, gently lifting her foot up as she leaned on me.

We chose a pair of shoes that resembled sneakers but were apparently not – I clearly didn't understand a thing about the clothes or shoes that girls wore. We were making our way back to the clothes section when I suddenly felt her fingers press hard into my side.

'I have to sit down,' she said in a trembling, weak voice. I could hear her breath clattering against her chest.

'Now?' I asked, looking around the crowded store.

'Yes.'

'Are you all right?'

She started coughing, deep coughs, like something was trying to claw itself out of her.

'I ... I just need to ... sit,' she wheezed.

I looked around desperately for a chair, a sofa, a stool but there was not a single place to sit – just rows and rows of clothes, and hundreds of disinterested people milling around.

'Stay right here,' I said. 'I'll go and find something and bring it here.'

I left her standing by the shoe counter, pale as a ghost, and I limp-ran to the cash counter. But there was no place to sit. I bumped into what felt like a hundred people as I clumsily made my way to the entrance of the store where a guard stood. I begged him to help. He waved me away lazily, telling me that there was no chair here.

In lieu of a chair, I desperately searched for water as if it were gold, but I couldn't find that either, till finally one of the salesgirls gave me her waterbottle and I rushed back where I had left Riya quavering like a leaf. But I didn't find her, not where I had left her standing next to a mannequin flaunting a florescent pink dress. I searched for her everywhere in the crowded store, my heart limping like my leg and in my panic, I felt revolted by my own heart, that pitiful weak muscle that pushed against my ribs.

Where could she have gone? I fought my way between the long racks of clothing, pushing through sari-clad aunties, to many disapproving coughs and glances. But everything looked the same. I wanted to shout her name, but my voice was stuck in my throat so I went round and round, dizzy with worry, thinking every girl with long brown, hair suddenly looked like her.

I'm not sure when – to me, in my mania, it seemed like hours but it must have only really been minutes – but a salesgirl came up to me, the same one whose waterbottle I held in my hand.

'Are you looking for your friend?' she asked.

'Yes,' I said, huffing frantically.

'She's over there,' she said, pointing to a corner beneath a row of handbags.

I found Riya sitting as still as a mannequin in a corner of the bustling store, her knees to her chest, her head on her knees, her head in her hands. I bent down and offered her the waterbottle, but she refused to take a sip.

'What's happening?' I tried my best to keep the fear from my voice.

'Give me a second,' she mumbled. 'I'm just taking rest.'

'Let's go home,' I said, giving her my hand.

When I touched her skin, I almost pulled it back – heat was steaming out of her as if she was cooking from inside.

She had an expression on her face that was new to me. Her mouth was open, her eyes wide, she was looking nervously ahead, backwards, to the side. Is it possible, I wondered, that she's afraid?

Holding my hand, she tried to get up but she struggled and fell back. I realized then that she did not have the strength to even stand up. Because I couldn't carry her myself, I asked frantically for help. A stocky man obliged, lifting her up as lightly as a doll. Riya would have hated being carried out of the store like a baby, but now she did not make a single sound of protest. The man put her on the back seat of the car as gently as one would a corpse, and she lay there, eyes open, silent as steel.

'Specs,' she murmured under her breath.

'Should we go to the hospital?' I asked, though it was silly, because of course I knew what she would say.

'No, no…' she groaned, squinting her eyes blurrily as if she was having trouble seeing me. 'I just need to rest. I want to go home and rest.'

I didn't want to argue with her and I didn't want to take this decision alone. So we drove back to school, me holding her head in my lap, as she meandered in and out of sleep.

We were almost turning the bend that would put us on the road straight to Residency School, when she opened her eyes, blinking slowly as if her eyelids were made of lead and in a trembling voice she told me, 'I think I'll just wear my uniform.'

13

B.P. WAS LIVID with Riya and me, but because he didn't want to say anything to her, he took out his anger on me.

'She could have died,' he shouted, stalking up and down his study, trembling slightly, as though bodily preventing himself from physically attacking me.

I thought to myself: she's going to anyway. But I didn't say this out loud. I wanted to tell him that it was she who wanted to go, that I had tried to stop her, that she had insisted. But I didn't tell him that either. I didn't have the strength or the energy to defend myself. It was easier to sit there silently and listen to his rant. And so even though many words sat on the tip of my tongue, I ended up saying only two.

'Sorry, sir,' I mumbled every time he paused to take a breath in between his roars.

Finally, when B.P. had yelled himself out, and I cautiously looked up from the spot on the floor where I had fixed my gaze, I saw that he had gone red in the face and there were tears streaming down his face.

B.P. crying. How could it possibly be? I was so puzzled that I just stared. He was the strongest man I knew, the man who had twice the strength of ordinary men, and here he was standing in front of me reminding me of someone like me.

We ended up cancelling the party. Riya was simply too unwell to go through the ordeal or so said the doctor whom B.P. was now consulting at the drop of a hat. Should she go for a walk? Should she wash her hair? Should she wear a sweater, or maybe two?

And it ended up being moot, because the day after her episode, the news of her illness finally leaked. I wasn't sure how it happened or when; I assumed that B.P. told the teachers, who then told some of the students, who then told everyone else.

I felt angry but also quite sad. This was our secret, Riya's and mine, and now the whole damn world was involved. I wasn't ready for it, and I was sure that Riya wasn't too. But I also knew that she didn't have much time left now and we couldn't possibly hide it any more.

I was suddenly very popular – in a different way than

when I was prefect. People with whom I had never interacted patted me on the shoulder and asked me in hushed whispers how she was. Suddenly everyone seemed to care about Riya, and people like Mrinalini, who had been jealous of her, who had even hated her, began expressing their concern. Once again, the Residency School rumour mills spun – leukaemia, a hole in the heart, TB, polio. It seemed Riya had all the diseases anyone had ever heard of all at once. I could have clarified it all, but everyone talking about her made me feel ill and I didn't really feel like saying anything at all.

Even Vikram came to ask me if what he had heard was true. Again, he leaned in the doorway of my study, as though unwilling to cross the threshold; wavering slightly to and fro.

'Yes,' I told him. 'It's true.'

When I saw his expression, I couldn't help but laugh: the big bully of Residency School, scared of something as ordinary as death.

74

RIYA HAD A lot of visitors. So many people came to see her – teachers, sports staff and students – that I wondered if the party would have been a good idea after all.

I felt a little left out. I'd been coming to see Riya at the same time every day for months; now I had to wait in line. She was always so tired by the time everyone had gone that she fell asleep instantly. I ended up sitting by her bed and reading a lot.

The visits became a blur, people came and went, but there was one visit I remembered in particular. It was a sad, splotchy, gloomy day and the sky was so grey that it looked like even the clouds were on the brink of tears. I was there, sitting on her doorstep, like I always did, when Vikram came to see her, looking greasy and pleased, holding a small box in his hands.

He saw me and looked a little surprised.

'Hi,' he said with something that resembled a smile. 'Can I see her?'

He didn't have to ask me, but I was glad that he had. 'She's inside,' I said, without moving from my position on the stairs.

He shuffled his feet and we both held our ground till finally I relented and made way for him. A part of me wanted to follow, to sit with them while they spoke. I could have easily done so, but I knew it would be odd, and I didn't want her to think that anything was amiss.

The clouds glowered and threatened while I sat on that stoop. They were there an awfully long time: far longer than anyone else had been. The hair stood up on the back of my neck and my skin crawled with irritation. I wished I had the courage to do what B.P. so often did, politely ask the visitor to leave, saying it was time for Riya to rest. But that was B.P. and this was me, and all I did was sit and shiver on the step, the dusk settling around me, the air reeking of rotting leaves.

Eventually Vikram came out. His eyes seemed unnaturally red. I wondered if he was drunk. I had seen him like this sometimes when he had had too much to drink. I noticed then that the small box wasn't with him. I realized with a start what anyone else would have immediately known: that it, of course, was a gift.

He left and I stayed but I didn't go inside her house.

Instead, I pottered around outside, wondering what it was that they had spoken about for so long and what he might have brought her. I really hoped that it wasn't a Walkman at least. I knew I could have asked her, and she would have told me too, but though I made some vague references, somehow I never did get around to it, and neither did she.

75

'ARE YOU PRAYING?' I asked Riya one day, surprised to see what appeared to be a small temple in her house – a few brass idols, some flowers and incense whose too-strong scent wafted into the air.

I expected some Riya-style remark: 'Specs, you wouldn't get it;' or, 'Specs, go back to chess.'

But she just shrugged and quietly said, 'I don't know what else to do.'

This made me pause and look up from the temple that I was examining.

'What do you mean?'

'Exactly what I said. The doctor says it helps and it kind of does. You should pray too,' she continued after a pause, looking squarely and seriously at me.

'Why? We've never prayed in our lives.'

'I have.'

I always felt slightly unsettled to discover evidence of Riya's private existence, before I knew her. 'You have? When?'

'When I was very young, and now when I'm very old.'

'Very old? You're sixteen.'

'Well, I'm going to die, Specs, and technically that makes me at the end of my life. So, in a way, I am very old.'

There she went again. I had no response; this was a typical Riya-style remark.

'Okay,' I conceded, 'I'll think about it, this praying thing.'

'No, Specs,' she said, gripping my hand with an urgency so unusual that I realized that this was something serious.

'Please listen to me.'

'Okay, anything you want. I'll pray,' I sighed.

'Why though?' I wondered out loud. If I was going to do this, I might as well know why.

'I don't know, Specs, but I think it's important. It just … it just feels like the right thing to do.'

'I've never known what that means,' I said, doubt written all over my face.

'You overthink things, Specs. Sometimes you've just got to feel. It's sort of like, during a race, when I am about to win, and I'm running at the right tempo, it just really feels right.'

So I began to pray. Riya handed me a small idol for my room and I slipped God in my pocket, wondering what I would do next. My first thought was people would laugh at me. The second was that I didn't care. And the third that they wouldn't actually laugh at me because everyone had these idols except for me.

I hadn't thought much about God, not since my parents died. Before that I had vague memories of my mother teaching me how to pray, sitting next to her on my knees, bringing my hands up to my chest. I remembered these things as I remembered almost everything about my mother: sweetly and sepia-tinted, like a long-faded photograph.

The truth that I didn't want to share with Riya was that I didn't think much of this praying business. Early on in my life, I had realized that it was hard work that finally paid off. I knew that if I practised a hundred sums, I would get a hundred marks. Praying, I wasn't so sure about. I saw the others pray – Vikram was particularly devout, especially before a game or a test – and it always struck me as deeply hypocritical and selfish. You only talk to God when you want something? Why would he want a devotee like that?

But I wouldn't be asking for anything. So I took the idol to my room and placed it on my desk, and then as I had once done with my mother, so many years ago, I closed my eyes, sat on my knees, brought my hands to my chest and I spoke to God, first tentatively and then with a little more intent. I told Him how I felt and then I systematically gave Him reasons why Riya should get better and why she should live. I didn't ask him for anything; I argued and reasoned with him and occasionally raised my voice. Sometimes I did this for so long that my knees turned black and blue, and my leg ached so badly I couldn't sleep. It actually did make me feel better. But she only got worse and worse.

16

I WALKED BACK to my dorm one mild winter night, the trees tumbling and tossing with a foamy whoosh, the air fresh and sweet, and all my favourite stars twinkling in the sky. This night had no right to be so beautiful, not when Riya was about to die.

I had taken a different route back home tonight. I wanted some time to clear my mind, and I found myself wandering around at the far end of campus, near the junior school houses and the nursery school. In my wandering, I happened to cross by the school temple, and I'm not sure why, but I took off my shoes and went inside.

I hadn't been inside that temple for at least ten years: it was one of the few buildings in this school where I hadn't spent much time. The temple was dark and cool, and smelt like a mix of dirty socks and camphor. There were no lights except candles which flickered like winter stars. The light threw weird shadows on the garlanded statues. In the darkness, I could not tell which deity was which.

I wasn't sure why I had even showed up here but now that I had, I decided that there wasn't anything for me to do but to pray. And so I began to pray. I prayed mostly for Riya, I prayed for me and I even prayed a bit for B.P. I prayed to the book gods who were always kind to me. I prayed to all the different gods I knew – there were so many gods, couldn't just one of them hear me?

A big brass bell hung from the ceiling, and I reached up and touched the frozen clapper. I began ringing the bell, first measuredly, like a dirge; then faster and faster, like a dervish, or a storm. I hauled on the rope with all my strength, something inside me snapping, my rage matching the intensity of the sound. I rang the bells with such fury that my fingers went numb. I wanted to break the bells. I wanted to break these statues, break them like they had broken me.

I rang and rang the bells till the sound dissolved into a

cacophonic blur. With each clang I cried out to them, 'Hear me! Hear me! Why aren't you listening to me, you meaningless pieces of stone?' I imagined the sound booming through the night: gong gong gong, over the cricket field, past the main building, the academic block and Ashok House. I wanted everyone to hear, to feel what I felt. I wanted to get people out of their beds. I wanted them to scratch their heads and peer out of the window and ask each other: What on earth is going on?

Gradually, the madness passed and I lay down exhausted on the cool marble floor, my forehead burning, my white shirt stuck to my skin.

My wild heart thumped against my chest and I'm glad that my ribcage held in my wild heart. A sort of fatigue passed over me and suddenly I was tired of being angry, of yelling in my head. What was the point? It wasn't getting me anywhere. Lots of people yelled at God every day – even the people who had nothing to yell at him about. *My marks are bad. Why did you do this to me, God? My mother died, why did you do this to me, God? I have cancer. Why did you do this to me, God?* There were probably more angry people out in the world than there were holy ones, and I didn't want to be either. I decided, as I lay on the floor, that I was tired of fighting. I knew that I simply had to stop.

That night, as I left the temple, the bells and statues sitting there so calm as if they were mocking me, I vowed never ever to pray again, at least not until some part of my prayer was answered. One hint, one whisper, one sign from above. But the next day I was back at the temple, praying with all my might, apologizing for my tantrum too. I went back because I had no one else to turn to and nowhere else to go. But it wasn't strictly out of necessity, something inside me urged me to go. I kept hearing Riya's voice in my head: 'It just feels right, Specs.' Somehow, I was starting to know what she meant.

11

SHE CRIED ONLY once during her illness, and she did it like she ran – precisely, gracefully, step by step. First, her dimpled chin quivered. Then her nose, and then her eyes. Then came the tears, slowly and then at a steady stream. The tears seemed simply to exude from her, like drops of rain.

I knew that I had to hold her, comfort her; to say something, do something. But I couldn't manage any of it. I just stared at that quivering chin and those dewy tears that sprung from her almond eyes.

I let her cry till she had had her fill. Tears, I knew from experience, were always limited – after the quota was over, you couldn't cry any more. She gradually quieted down, and came and sat down next to me, quiet and quivering, hiccupping, her head resting on the right side of my arm.

I looked at her face and realized that she was scared. Riya, who never got scared. I was the craven, the coward, never ever her, and when she professed her fear to me in an unfamiliar, vulnerable voice, tears pricked my eyes. I held them back, though I almost choked. I was not strong, but I had to at least pretend to be. It occurred to me that the only thing more painful than crying was trying to hold back the tears.

Eventually, when my Adam's apple stopped throbbing and I could breathe steadily I reached out to her and held her in my arms. She put her chin on my shoulder and sniffled in my ear. We were almost the same height, and it felt good to hold her close like this, to feel her warmth across my chest.

For a long time we just sat there on her veranda. I, very still, trying to control the tears, while Riya, rid of hers, stared into the nothingness of space.

By now the last rays of sunshine had dissolved and the cold pierced us strong and hard.

'Specs,' she finally said. 'What's going to happen to me?'

I wanted to say something, but I couldn't answer that question without lying or crying or sounding totally dumb, so I didn't say anything at all. The irony, of course, was that this was all I thought about, day and night, the answers swarming around my head like drunken flies.

78

AS RIYA GREW weaker, for the first time since I had known her, she let herself be dependent on me. She allowed me help her sit up, help her walk, sometimes even help her get dressed. I would help her take off the thick, heavy woollen sweater, and then the thin T-shirt underneath, deliberately looking away from her chest, which was now as flat as a junior school girl's. Then I would comb her hair. This became a favourite ritual of mine, though it wasn't as easy as it seemed. I would brush her hair as gently as I could, concentrating almost as hard as I did on a maths sum, trying not to hurt her as I untangled the knots with my fingers and brushed it till it shone. Her hair was always soft and sweet-smelling and thick, like rich dark loam, vital and healthy, even as she faded. And it always smelled like the earth.

Physical contact, which I thought irritated her when she was healthy, she now seemed to like. She touched me more, held my hand, drew me into her embrace. She would cling to me, softly rubbing my sleeves or hair as if she wanted to slip inside me and stay there.

It was worse when her mind began playing tricks on her – she would start speaking and then suddenly forget what she was about to say, instead coughing in scared ragged fits. She didn't especially want visitors now, though people still came. She would hardly see anyone at all. I would come every day and even though I just sat and she just slept, she would do so facing me: so we could be together for as long as we could possibly be.

When I wasn't with her, I was in a daze. I attended classes but didn't hear a thing. I read my books but didn't understand a word. I even did my homework but didn't register anything. Most people left me alone, and when they tried to speak to me, I replied though I never quite remembered the conversations that we had. Vikram, strangely quiet and not quite as smug as before, asked me more often than I would have liked how she was. I tried my best to accept everything, and even though I almost had, there still remained a tiny fragment of hope.

I guess as long as there is life there is hope, and I hoped endlessly for a miracle. But nothing happened, and as each day went by, she spent more time sleeping, falling deeper into her illness as I looked on, not able to do a thing. Imagine watching the person that you love most fade, while you continue to live, and I wished for the thousandth time that I could give my life for hers.

19

WE WERE SITTING on the sofa in the living room, her feet propped in my lap. I had just failed the first exam in my life – physics, electromagnetic waves – but strangely I had not felt anything except nostalgia when I looked at my answer sheet marked red and remembered Riya's old maths exams.

'If there was anything that you could do right now what would it be?' I asked, tickling her toes.

She didn't think about it for even a second, which meant that she had thought about it a lot. 'I miss running,' she said. 'It was what made me feel alive.'

I didn't say anything for a long time, I only thought and then I looked at her, beatific in the light of the lamp, so thin, so pale, so fragile that she seemed almost invisible.

'Well, let's do it, then. Let's run.'

She shrugged and looked away. 'How? I can't. And you can't either. One thing that we finally share.'

'My calamity and your fate,' I murmured automatically, rubbing her ankles carefully.

'Have you been reading Shakespeare again?'

'Maybe,' I said a little embarrassed.

She gave me a look that suddenly pierced me, it was so typically her: how many more of those will I ever see?

'I'm going to take you running,' I said with false resolve.

'Have you been reading love stories again?'

'No,' I said a little offended now. 'Let's go, it'll be fun.'

She didn't look convinced.

'It's beautiful outside. Your gods have given us summer for just one day.'

She still didn't look convinced so I tried again. This time, I decided, I wouldn't let it go.

'Remember that time you wanted me to ride the bike?'

She nodded her head.

'Well, I did, didn't I? Even though I'd never imagined being on a bike.'

'Now you're Superman on that bike,' she said, remembering with a little smile on her pale lips.

'I did what you asked me to do, and now you have to do what I say.'

And she did. We slipped off to the track, me in a tracksuit and a crippled leg, she in a night suit and a wheelchair, a shawl covering her legs. I had no idea what I was doing, but I knew that I had to make this happen, no matter what.

The weather, at least, was on my side. The cold had broken and a gentle, fragrant breeze blew through the night. It was really as if the weather gods had thawed winter just for this night.

I had pushed the heavy metal wheelchair all the way to the track from Riya's house, almost a kilometre or more. My chest was heaving and I was drenched in sweat. Now I stood there, in the quiet of the night, realizing that somehow I had to run.

I had till now never run, not even once in my life. I had

limped, walked, stumbled. I had fallen and crawled. I had even cycled, but I had never really run. I took off my glasses and closed my eyes, the white chalked lines fading into a blur and I suddenly launched myself from a standstill, pushing the wheelchair with all my crippled might. Leaning most of the weight of my body against the wheelchair, I pushed her and myself onto the track, and my legs had no option but to explode into movement. I started erratically, wildly, slowly before an ancient human instinct came into play, gaining momentum step by step, somehow my legs not just keeping up, but propelling us on. Then she released the gears of the wheelchair and bent forward at the waist, her mouth slightly open, exactly as she did when she ran. We went faster and faster, my legs for once obeying my heart, moving fervently, more decisively than they had ever before. Then in a heartbeat, before I could fathom what was going on, I was running. I was really running and the wind was in her hair as I ran and we spun and she flew. And just like that, I, who had never run before, finally ran for the first time in his life.

80

THE DAY BEGAN ominously. I slept fitfully and when I woke up, the world seemed oddly empty and silent and I realized that the birds that created havoc in the morning were today as silent as stones. I felt in the pit of my stomach that something was wrong and I lay in bed, lost in my uncomfortable fog, missing assembly and not even making it to my first class. The feeling stayed through Singh Ma'am's double-period physics class, as she droned on about the Heisenberg Uncertainty Principle. I tried really hard to focus – this was my favourite topic after all – but it was impossible to ignore the discomfort in my heart, and my mind kept straying to her, no matter what.

The feeling persisted through tea break, through chemistry, through biology and through maths. I became nervous though I didn't know why, I squirmed in my seat and I shook my good leg so hard that I moved the desk. I spilled ink on my fingers and looked at page fifty-nine while the teacher read from sixty-two. I stared out of the window at the oppressively bright day, squinting as the sunlight reflected like spears on the huge paint-splashed panes of glass, the trees so green, everything too still, too bright, too perfect to be real.

Finally, when I couldn't take it any more, when my mind felt like it may just explode, I got up in the middle of the English class and without even asking the teacher, I made my way out of the door, my footsteps echoing loudly in the empty corridors. I walked over to B.P.'s office where the wooden door was bolted shut. I rattled the handle uselessly, wondering where he was. I knew that today was Monday, the day of the senior staff meeting, and even with Riya's illness, this was not something that B.P. could miss. I went next to Principal Sir's office where his mean-faced, octogenarian secretary gave me a cold stare. Typically, I would have run off in fright, but today I didn't care and I asked him if B.P. was there. He didn't say a word and just made a face, and bobbed his head left and right, which I knew meant a no. I went next to the senior teachers' parking lot next to the main building, looking for B.P.'s white car, but it was nowhere in sight. The day had fooled me – though it was bright, it was cold as ice. I hadn't brought my coat, but I hurried as fast as I could towards her house.

By the time I reached, I was panting and my glasses were frozen to my face. I saw that there was no car outside and when I edged closer I saw a padlock on the door. They had never, as long as I had known her, once locked the door. For a moment, my heart stood still and then a strange fear, stronger than anxiety, stronger than sorrow, stronger than anything I had known, overtook me and thrashed furiously inside my chest.

The air was so cold now it was hard for me to breathe but I knew that I had to get to the hospital. I limp-ran the three kilometres to the main gate, lifting and dragging my stupid leg when it cramped in bone-numbing pain. At the school gate, the guards looked at me curiously and I panted for breath, the taste of blood in my mouth.

'Auto … auto,' I said but they looked dumbly into the distance with not a single auto in sight.

There was no option but to turn around and go back, to somehow find a way from the school to the hospital. I walked fast, pulling my leg behind me, my shoe scraping the gravel, though I couldn't feel a thing. And then I fell hard, snot in my mouth, each breath now fire in my chest. I got up and continued but then I fell again. And again. And again. When I couldn't walk any more, not a single step, I sat on the side of the road, white, breathless, my glasses cracked from my fall, so desperate now that I thought about crawling back.

I saw a boy sauntering towards me from the distance, and even in my pain, and through the cracks, I recognized him: there was no one else with a walk like that. He was the last person in the world that I would have liked to see, but there he was mid-class, out on the 'prefect duties' that should have been mine.

He looked at me curiously, no jeer on his lips.

'Is everything all right?' he asked, almost sounding concerned.

'Riya…' I managed to say, the fire in my chest burning bright as I wiped my dripping nose.

'Is she okay?' he asked, now with an edge in his voice.

No, my mind screamed, but I managed one word. 'Hospital.'

I sat there looking up at him, and he looking down at me. And in that silent exchange he understood what I was trying to say – it must have been those twelve long years we had shared.

'Wait. We need a car,' he slowly said, his bushy eyebrows knitting like caterpillars above his beady eyes.

I nodded. He told me to wait, and sprinted like a gazelle as I sat there holding my frozen leg. He was back in minutes, zipping down the road in a cherry-red car. For a second, I thought he wouldn't stop but then he braked, the tyres screeching, almost running over my good leg.

He got out of the car, gave me his hand and helped me into the car.

'Is this Principal Sir's car?' I asked.

'Yes,' he said, a tense smile on his face.

'You…'

'Stole it,' he finished the sentence as we sped out of the gate, the guards grinning widely as they saluted him.

81

SOMETHING ABOUT THE blue-white light in Riya's room intensified everything – the starkness of the walls, the whiteness of the sheets, the steel-grey of the machines that were attached to almost every single part of her. Nurses, doctors swarmed around her and B.P. sat by her side. His face had not changed but his lips were white; he just sat there looking at her, blinking very fast.

Riya lay there, tiny and flat like a little girl, an insubstantial wrinkle under the sheet. Her body scarcely sunk into the bedding, her closed eyes shrunken twin circles, the mauve shadows on her body telling of sleepless nights, the creases between her brows speaking of silent pain.

I stood outside her room for a long time, just waiting and watching everything and everyone. Gradually, the doctors and nurses left, talking in hushed whispered and murmuring tones. Only B.P. was left now, sitting by her side, not staring at her any more but straight out in front, caressing her cheekbones. Then in an act of tenderness – which almost seemed unnatural for such a severe and stern man – he kissed her gently on the eyes.

I entered the room now. We did not speak but looked at each other in the halogen lights cast from the machines. For a moment, I thought of what I looked like to him – my pants torn at the knees, my glasses cracked, my sweater streaked with dirt, snot and blood, but then I looked at Riya and all thoughts vanished from my head. For a second, she opened her eyes and they were clouded as if covered by a thin membrane. She looked at something somewhere, maybe even me, but then she closed her eyes, sliding back into another world. I didn't have to ask him what was going on. Even without saying a word, we both knew that she was dying and that this was the end.

82

I PROVED TO be a tender nurse, sitting with her through the worst of it, holding her hand that went cold and then warm. Her wrists were so thin and fragile that even when I held them gently I was afraid that they would snap. B.P. was there too, speaking to the nurses, the doctors, whoever came and went, but I sat there, on a small plastic chair, not moving an inch, not paying any heed to them, not hearing a thing except for what she occasionally said.

She whispered to me like the red munia, my favourite musical bird that sang as if it was always short of breath. There was something so gentle and sad in her feeble song, there was no sound to me more lovely in the world.

'Specs…' she whispered.

And then her voice broke in a raspy cough.

'Yes, yes,' I said in a hushed tone. 'Don't worry, it will be all right.'

Then a little while later, who knew how long – maybe minutes, maybe hours because I had lost all track of time what seemed like a long while ago – 'Specs,' she said. 'Your specs.'

I touched the crack in my glasses. I could swear that even now she was teasing me, that there was a glimmer of a grin on her thin pale face.

While I sat there with her, day stretched into dusk, the blue broke into black, the rain turned into hail and the sound of it, like bullets against my chest, kept me awake even as my bones ached with exhaustion, and my body craved for sleep.

At some point I fell asleep – a light gauzy sleep – and when I awoke with a start, I found that I had fallen over, and somehow my head had landed right next to her chest. I opened my eyes, her face so close to mine, and from where I was she seemed not to have aged, but to have become young, like she was eight or nine. Her arms and legs had been reduced to weeds, her hair, as wild as it ever had been, was caught in her eyes and her mouth. I moved it away, a familiar gesture by now; then, for a second, she opened her eyes and looked into mine. And for a moment before she closed her eyes, I felt as if we were the only two souls in this world.

Then B.P. came and shook me out of my reverie. He gruffly told me to go downstairs and get something to drink. I walked out of the hallway, wandering and weaving like a drunk, descending the two flights of steps down to the main lobby of the hospital. There I spotted him, exactly where I had left him sitting on a flimsy chair. Seeing the sleeping bodies lying around, I realized that it was the middle of the night. He was there, I couldn't understand why.

Principal Sir's car, I thought vaguely, somewhere in some part of my brain.

'How is she?' he asked.

I didn't say a word, just shook my head. There was no point in lying now.

He didn't say anything either but stared at me with terrified eyes. He nodded vaguely, and ran his hand through his hair several times. Then he cleared his throat and mumbled to me, 'I called the house. Told them that you won't be coming. To arrange a night pass.'

I wanted to say something to him, maybe thank you, but I just looked at him numbly, not saying a word.

He handed me a bottle of water. I took it and left.

83

HOW QUICKLY SHE died. How fast it was over.

At some point in the night, it began to snow. Till now there had been lightning and thunder but no snow, but the sky had now given in finally to the weight of the ice. I remember watching the flakes coming down from the thick panes of glass, piling on the windowsill.

The master had told me what to do. He had told me to speak to her, to pray, not to leave her side at the end. I whispered things in her ear, 'Your suffering has a purpose, a far greater purpose than you will ever know. Dedicate this suffering with all your heart to all those who are in pain. Breathe in their suffering, breathe out well-being and healing for other souls.'

B.P. came, the nurses and doctors too. Some asked me to leave, if I argued, I didn't quite remember, I didn't get up and go. I sat there, imploring those dark eyes, drowsy with death, the small mouth still fighting pain, for breath to stay. I wanted to say to her, to shake her shoulders and to scream. 'Make an effort to live, Riya, make an effort to live.'

But I knew that I had to let her go easily, without tears, without sorrow without a fight, and so I continued whispering to her the things the master had said.

Right before she passed away, it was a peculiar feeling. She sighed once and stretched, as if finally comfortable. Nothing changed but something did and I knew by holding her hand that now, now it was finally time. That is what I had always imagined, and this is what it finally was.

Her face seemed to give off a glow, reminding me of the silvery moon at its glorious best, on the clearest and coldest of winter nights. She was luminous, as if her soul had risen very close to the surface and was lighting her skin. At first, I thought I was dreaming, but even after I rubbed my eyes, it was still there, a blaze of a rainbow that seemed to be radiating from the crown of her hair.

Ever so slowly, she opened her heavy, heavy eyes. 'Specs,' she whispered in a faint, flat voice.

Damn it, even now. At least at the end, she could call me by my name. But this, I knew, was no time to argue or to make this point.

'If I could wish for one thing.'

'You can … you can,' I said, my voice desperate and hushed as I smoothed her hair with my palm.

'I wish,' she said in a tiny whisper, each word filled with pain.

Silence fell and in her face there were signs of struggle as she gathered strength to speak again.

'I wish to spend my next life with you.'

With those words, her voice faltered into stillness, the words evaporated into the air, and the girl I loved more than love itself died with me sitting by her side.

84

B.P. CAME, THE doctors came, and people rushed into the tiny room. There was a long beep that stung my ears, it was the sound that I heard above all other sounds. I heard it for days afterward, ringing so loudly that I would wake up with a start in the middle of the night. As people crowded around me into the room, there was no place for me, so I left and roamed the halls of the hospital aimlessly. I didn't know where I was going but at some point I found myself downstairs and Vikram was still waiting in that chair.

He saw me and rushed up to me.

'How is she?' he demanded. 'What's happening?'

I stared at him blankly. He looked at me, very tired and suddenly he was a little boy, just like he had been when we were six. I hadn't said a word but he knew exactly what had passed. And then each part of his face seemed to collapse, slowly one by one. First his eyes, then his nose, then his cheeks and then his mouth, and he just stood there, his mouth open wide in shock. For once, his eyes were unmasked and in them I saw the helplessness and bewilderment that reflected my very own.

Then, just like that, it all faded and everything got crushed and I stared at him numbly and he broke into tears. He bent forward and pressing his palms and knees on the floor, he began to cry on all fours. I had never in my life seen anyone cry with such intensity and I reached out and placed a hand on his trembling back. Then I crouched beside him and held his head gently as he cried.

85

HE IS EXACTLY as I have imagined he would be – smouldering eyes beneath jutting brows, hooked nose with flaring nostrils, a petulant, mean mouth. Pompous, loud, arrogant and bald, walking with that careless gait – still an athlete, after all these years. Over the years, he has gained weight, but even now I can see through his well-tailored clothes that his body is muscular and taut, and that he has the same bold insolence in his eyes.

We exchange platitudes: he congratulates me on my success, I on his, he asks me about my family and I ask about his. Then, as if it were the most natural thing in the world, as if we were simply old friends meeting after a long time, he says that he is starving and if the food here is anything like it used to be, we should get away from here.

Johnny Hot Dog, Residency School's favourite joint, still existed, still operated by the obese Chugan Lal standing at the corner of Chapan dukan. A modern facade, a big sign, new chairs, an extension, but the menu remained the same. They still sold banjos, a sort of hot dog with egg that every boy in Residency School used to love. We sit down on a table, order and then we are exchanging pleasantries about our careers and life trajectories.

After school, Vikram had gone to a top college in Delhi under the sports quota, where he had a glorious career in hockey, being big man on campus, playing nationals, partying like a prince and cosying up with women, till he met his future wife. He implies – in fact, does explicitly state – that he still has a wandering eye. He then did an MBA in the US where he had travelled, hung out at bars, worked at an investment bank and had his son about the same time as I had mine. He returned to India five years ago to join his father's burgeoning business where he had recently led the IPO.

The banjos arrive and I stare at my plate, and it all looks slightly gross – the too red-hot sauce, the chutney so green that it almost shines. Flies swarm around us, settling on anything moist, and we wave our hands and flick our napkins. Neither of us touch our rolls. Vikram talks almost nonstop, grinning arrogantly, aware that he is dominating me – and aware that I am aware of this. As we sit there, the voice I hear is not of the man sitting in front of me but of a taunting, jeering fifteen-year-old. Though so many years have passed, I realize that the dynamics between us have not changed at all.

He must have read my thoughts because we suddenly lapse into an uncomfortable silence and sit there playing with our plastic spoons, nudging our rolls, wincing at the bright light of the blue skies and the mountains that rise all around us like sharp teeth. I rack my brain for things to say and I open my mouth to speak some banality but then he begins to speak.

He speaks slowly as if he has practised his words. 'You know, I was always so jealous of you.'

I look up, startled, his voice has no more expression than his face.

Him, jealous of me?

I am strangely amused. 'Why?' I say with a hard laugh.

His lips curl and he turns his swarthy head away. 'You seemed to have a good life, away from our mess.'

I think to myself: *What life? The life of an orphan? Of a scholarship student?* I say nothing, sensing he wants to continue.

He does. He cracks the knuckles of his right hand. 'A life without your father's pressure, without the burden of a legacy. A life in which you didn't have to play a role, or pretend, or act.'

This surprises me. 'You were acting?'

'Every hour of it,' he says right away. 'Every minute. Except sometimes.'

Except sometimes. I know where this is going. I am determined not to talk about her with him.

'I never knew,' I say cautiously. 'I'm sorry to hear that.'

What else could I possibly say?

He nods absently.

We look at our untouched rolls, drowning in red sauce, black flies like pepper flakes.

I shoo them away with my hand.

'Plus, you had her. And I didn't,' he says. His voice is low and he doesn't look directly at me, but stares out at the trees on his left, the tip of his tongue curled over his softly trembling lip.

I remember that expression. It is classic Vikram. In the middle of the exams in which I snuck him notes, when he scored his famous goals, when he ran a race. Oh, I remember that look – of Vikram focusing very hard.

'Riya,' I say, swallowing hard.

He takes a deep breath, then exhales. There is a weird lump in my throat – awfully familiar, but also unknown, like some sort of ancient instinct that I recognize vaguely from many years ago.

God. Not here, not now, not in front of him.

'She loved you. And … that's all I ever wanted. Riya. But she was the one thing I could never have.'

I have no words for him, I just look him in the face, and suddenly so many things make sense to me. I have been such a blind fool – how couldn't I have known when it was always there staring me in my face?

And then as clear as if it was just yesterday, I remember, them on the race track, him following as she led, them standing in the hallway, she smiling, books to her chest. I remember the way he had looked when he had walked out of her house without the gift, how he had wept that night at the hospital. The memories come like a torrent and sweep me away. I can't handle it, not all at once. I get up from my chair unsteadily, I fish through my pocket for some bills, throw them on the table and then without a word I walk away.

He had driven us here, and now I walk the uphill path back – the shortcut that runs through Dhobi Ghat – as hard for me now as it was back then, especially since my leg now hurts as badly as if I was seventeen again, running down that road, desperate to get to Riya at the end.

I sit down on a rock, catching my breath, and the cold air stings my chest. He had loved Riya, desired her, probably for the same reasons as I. She had meant something to him, as she had to me. He had experienced her in a way that I never had, running by her side. How could this be? I hold my face in my hands, feeling the wet streaks of sweat, my head going round and round and round. I am suddenly exhausted and then I remember how it had been at the end.

86

A BURNING BODY has a peculiar smell, it's a smell that you can never forget and there is absolutely nothing to compare it with. The clothing catches first, then the hair begins crisping; the skin melts suddenly, and then go the bones. But not the soul. That is already gone.

Here I am, all these years later, the same spot on campus surrounded by boys dressed in white. The funeral ground is vast and empty, located next to Dhobi Ghat, the clouds today are white and narrow as bones, the sky wide open, the horizon extending as far as the eye can see.

B.P. was beloved. There were a lot of people back then, and a lot of people now. Today, as that day, her badge that hung around my neck, next to my heart, glows like burning coals. Today, as that day, I stand frozen, feeling nothing but the beads of sweat that trickle down my neck. Then, as now, I am surrounded by my batchmates but distinctly set apart; they crowd together in little herds and these thirty-something-year-old men are suddenly fourteen again.

I am successful, and they know it too. But despite everything, I feel so small again, like a crippled boy who is just a ghost. Vikram stands there, dressed in white, his eyes burning like the fire, the flames dancing in fright. He had loved her too, maybe as much as me. I never knew what had happened, I never knew what was in that box.

I stand there, staring at the burning fire, holding my breath till I get dizzy and the blood rushes to my face. Time splits and refracts, as though through broken glass. Sixteen years, six months, eight days. I want to forget, but I cannot. The maths, the numbers always come to me, floating in my brain, swirling in my head and suddenly I'm there again as if it's yesterday.

87

I HADN'T SEEN her body, I was afraid to go up close. They say she wore one of her mother's old saris, that she had been dressed by relatives she had never met. A games uniform would have been more appropriate, I hazily thought.

The whole batch had gathered, even though she hadn't been close to any of them. There was so many little hypocrisies: teachers who had belittled her now praised her aptitude; girls who had ignored her ostentatiously sobbed on each other's shoulders. Her coaches talked about her work ethic and grit. No one knew what she really was: a gust of wind, perfectly free.

But I was in no state to protest – I was numb and I didn't know what to do any more. After she died, I had flitted in and out. I didn't know what was happening most of the time and the days passed by in a blur. At Riya's funeral, I remember that someone had had to loan me a white kurta – maybe it was Vikram, who was strangely vigilant. He organized memorials, prayers, vigils, his leadership skills in full play. I too was there at them, although I don't remember a single thing.

Before they carried her body to the pyre, B.P. called me, motioning for me to come with a jerk of his head. Stiffly, in a trance, I obliged. Up close I saw that his face had aged a million years. He had the sunken face of an old man, haggard and carved. In the distance somewhere I heard a silent, agonizing wail.

Carrying her body on my shoulder, I got a brief glimpse. Though there was a body there was no life. A dead body was, after all, dead. It wasn't Riya, though she was still all there. This was not my girl, but someone else, shrivelled and very old.

I had never seen a body burn before. What went first was the hair, her long hair, her messy hair. The fire was surprisingly noisy, it sounded like it was eating Riya's body, greedily smacking its lips. I stood there entranced by the dancing flames, and I remembered what Monty Sir, the chemistry teacher had said – it's the hair that causes a burning body to smell. As I saw her body burn, a column of white smoke rising up, I swear I saw something sparkle above the burning mass and float away with the clouds.

And then it was over, as quickly as it had begun, and then there was nothing left of my glorious girl with her long legs and her wild hair and her sweet face, strong as I would never know strength again. People patted each other's backs and murmured their condolences to B.P. I suddenly understood something that had been in my mind, just out of reach. Riya, she was never of this world. She was never meant to be caged. Holding on to her forever would have been impossible – she was born to run, to fly, to soar. Now she was finally free.

I was the last to leave the ground. I stood there for many hours, next to the burning wood and the dying embers.

When B.P. asked me to come, 'Later,' I softly said.

He understood because he left me alone, standing there, surrounded by her ashes like fairy dust. Then the vultures came, and then the sweepers, gathering away the rest of her remains and then it was nightfall and then the sky turned from blue to grey.

88

I REMAIN AS the rest of them flit away, the smoke twine in lazy languorous tendrils, the ashes like confetti in the wind. If she had been alive, what would have been?

'Specs, the life you have is the life you are meant to live.'

How many times have I repeated this line over and over to myself, especially in the years after she died?

I wonder though, was I living my life? A good life? A happy life? I am successful, I have a son and I love him; I have a wife and I love her too – not in the way I loved Riya, but in another way. But was I living the best life that I possibly could? The life I would have lived if I had thirty days to live? The life that she had wanted me to live? I remember the book she had once given me, *The Man Who Knew Infinity*, and then she had whispered into my ear, 'You're a genius too.'

I had once held infinity in my palm but I had to release it now as I had back then. She rescued me now as she had done back then and as I stand, the fire burning bright, I know that she would never have wanted me to be the way I have become. I decide in that moment that I have to change my life.

After another hour, I walk away, the ground sodden and swampy, the sky unfurling its clouds. I have almost reached the road when I hear a shrill cry. I turn around and see a tiny, shrivelled figure approaching me. I squint my eyes, and wonder if it could really be him.

'Bhaiyya!' he yells in a raspy old voice.

It is undoubtedly him, as crumpled as he had ever been, limping towards me with a toothless grin.

'Jeevan,' I whisper to the wind.

How happy I am to see this ancient man alive.

'Bhaiyya!' he cries, folding his hands as I pull him up, bringing him to my chest.

'Jeevan,' I say as I hold the frail old man close. He smells of the mountains, of wood smoke. How old must he be? A hundred? A hundred and two?

'For you,' he rasps, shoving a small bag in my hands.

Apparently, B.P. had found it just a few days before he had died. They had tried mailing it to me, but the courier had been returned. I realize that the school must have had my grandparents' address but they passed away a long time ago, and I had sold their property for the down payment on my house.

I stare hard at the bag and then I open it. My breath catches, my heart seems to flip. I am a grown man with a wife and a son, MD at India's biggest bank. But here I am once again, feeling just like a crippled little boy.

It is from Riya and inside is a letter and a small black box.

89

I HAD TWO options after she died. I could give up or I could live on.

I chose to live on because that is what she would have wanted, that is what she had asked. I could not limp away from my life any more than Riya could run away from hers. People learned to live with things and this was my life. I had to learn how to live with it, even if it was now a miserable, messy affair. I knew with more surety than anything else that I was dying, as was everyone else on Earth, and so I had to learn how to live.

Before I knew her, though I hadn't quite understood it, I lived almost entirely inside my head. But she had taught me to live in the present – this was her greatest gift to me – and I knew that I had to go on, and to accept what was coming my way.

I didn't have much time left after she died, and suddenly I wanted to get away from the place that I had earlier never wanted to leave. It was Riya who had dreamt of leaving, never me. I had been happy to be here at Residency School, the only world I had known, puttering in my little room, creeping in the old halls and the hidden nooks. But without her, the world that I had known was shattered and nothing was the same any more. So I made a promise to myself and to her that I would leave, I would get out of here and go to a better place. Nowhere would be better without her, but I didn't want to be that loser, that wimp, I wanted to be something better, someone of whom she would be proud.

The days passed, the seasons turned, the twelfth-standard board exam chaos started again. I watched my classmates, my juniors, my teachers all around me stressing, studying, worrying. They were all kind to me, leaving me mostly alone. They didn't even come ask me for my notebooks, because everyone knew that they were incomplete. Vikram too let me be, nodding his head at me as he passed me by. I looked at him blankly, gazed right through him, like I did with the rest.

During the day I locked myself in my small room, thinking only of my books and of her. I had seen her body turn to ash, but I still couldn't adjust to the fact that she had returned to nothingness. It was too strange to think that she was no longer a part of this world. So I didn't. I studied and studied till nothing made sense any more, my grief and sadness melting into my books.

But at night when I lay down dog-tired, my head spinning with numbers and formulae, I would close my eyes and walk into another life. We were back in the eleventh standard. I would wake up and daydream my way through class. The games bell would ring and I would make my way to the track, and there amongst the clouds and chalk, I would watch her run, as graceful as a bird in flight.

I would bike my way to her house, the wind blowing in my hair, the trees dense and green, and I would end up with her on the doorsteps of her house in the light of the fading sun. In those days I often thought of what the master had said –

celebrate death like you do life. But no matter how much I tried, I couldn't get myself to celebrate her death.

But I did do something.

I went to the place that she loved most, the track, and next to the pavilion, in a small patch of mud, I sprinkled her ashes and planted a tree. Then I found some marigold seeds and I sprinkled those in the sodden earth too.

Now when I return all those years later, there it is in the distance, close to the finish line – a tree, brown bark, green leaves and very much a tree. It is surrounded by a spark of overgrown orange marigolds that cover parts of the track, so bright that they hurt the eye. These flowers are different from anything else on campus where flowers were planted neatly in beds around the school, colour-coordinated to match houses and walls. These are wild, disorderly, growing haphazardly around a solitary, misplaced tree. It is all so enchanting that even the Residency School's militaristic malis did not have the heart to tear them down. As I look, I see a pair of lovers go sit underneath that tree.

I smile to myself, thinking that all is as it should be. They would carve their names on the walls of lovers and then go sit in a bed of marigolds, and kiss under the tree.

As for B.P., we never spoke again. There was no specific reason for this. He was involved in his grief and I in mine. I often saw him in the distance, coaching in his cricket whites, blowing his whistle loudly, sometimes in the hallway in his suit. Once, I caught him staring blankly at the board of school captains and prefects where Riya's name was carved in gold, and where mine had recently been replaced by Vikram's upon his request.

When I graduated, he patted me heartily on the back, congratulated me with a beam like he did with every single boy, nothing more and nothing less.

I wanted to say goodbye to him before I left campus. So, after my last exam, I biked to the house, but without Riya on the steps, I cycled back as fast as I could to pack up the rest of my things, before I left, once and for all, the campus that had been my home for twelve years.

Yet.

Yet.

Not a day, a minute, a moment passed by when I didn't think of her, when she wasn't with me by my side. I don't care what people say, but I swear she was there every step of the way. The day I sat stuck on that exam, quietly encouraging me to answer the final question, the one which only eighteen students in the country got correct.

'Come on, Specs, you know this! Don't be so dumb.'

I swear she was there with me, graduating, throwing her cape in the air.

I swear she was there when I sat for the last time on the steps of Scindia Pavilion, quietly sobbing by myself.

And then she was there when I finally left, just like she was when I first saw her, so glorious that she took my breath away, a miracle, an apparition, her short, white socks, her dusty black shoes, that ponytail that swirled in the wind.

As I sat at the back of the taxi, I turned around, and there she was at the big metal gates of Residency School, waving to me as I left.

She didn't stop me when I was leaving, just like I didn't stop her when she was. Instead, she stood there, a smile on her face, telling me, 'Go, Specs, go. Go make a life that you'll be proud of. Go have adventures where they are to be had, and never for a second, a minute, look back into the past and be sad.'

And as the car took the bend, she whispered in my ear, 'I am with you every step of the way.'

I knew then that leaving was simply a journey back to her.

90

NOW, I HAVE time to write. I am working on a schoolbook of mathematics, something I have always wanted to do. My wife, she's now in charge, I hear her gentle voice, giving stern orders as everyone follows her command. Believe it or not, but we left the city and became farmers, organic farmers. We are happy here, our kids are growing up well, and Meeta is unbelievably good at what she does. Back in the city, she couldn't find her feet, but she loves it here – she is the one who runs the show.

My son went to boarding school this year. We didn't send him to Residency School. It's still high on the rankings, and Meeta was keen, but I knew that I couldn't go back – not three times a year, not where the past was so real. Instead, we sent him to one of those new-age boarding schools, which, believe it or not, doesn't even have a school uniform.

My daughter has woken up now.

'Papa?' she says in a sleepy voice.

'Yes, jaan?'

She rubs her twinkling eyes.

'Is it time yet?'

I look at my watch – 4.00 p.m.

'You were supposed to wake me up.'

'Sorry, my love. Your papa, he got lost.'

But she isn't listening, not right now. She hops up from the sofa, throws on her sneakers, and holding my fingers tight we walk to the track.

Three minutes later, she's flying down that track, her little arms and legs like a songbird in flight. State trials are next week, and my little Riya, she is determined to win, determined to break all records, though most are already hers.

I stand there, stopwatch in my hand, watching her run, and all of a sudden, I see a flurry of dust rising on the tracks, and there she is calling out my name, her blue skirt flying behind her, her hair wild in the wind. She is so real that I reach out to touch her, and it's really as if she is there, and I am there, and in that moment, I realize once again what it is like to be absolutely and wholly complete.

91

SPECS,

By the time you get this letter I will not be alive. But I wanted you to know a couple of things so here it is – the first letter I have written in my life. I know you like it here, but if you stay here, you will end up just like Ansari Sir. I don't think you want that and neither do I. I think you should end up more like Ramanoojem (however, you spell his name) than him.

I want you to go out, to do wonderful things and to discover your infinity like I discovered my own. I want you to live as if you only had thirty days to live. Remember what the master said? I was, I am, we are all going to die. What I did at the end, I want you to do now. Begin the process of becoming the person that you want to be when you die.

Life can be snatched away from us at any moment – you know that better than I – so all we can really do is to live each moment the best that we can. I want you to do that, Specs, I really do. I know that you will then find as much peace, grace, love and happiness as this world allows. You may be feeling lonely and sad. But I want to tell you that the entire universe is within you, and inside that universe there is also me.

I love you, Specs. Remember that I am with you, always, by your side.

Love,

Riya

P.S. Vikram gave me this. I never opened it. I wanted you to have it, whatever it is that is inside.

I opened the creaky lid of the small black box and there it was glittering like fool's gold, my prefect badge, which had seen numbered days pinned to my chest. Vikram had taken it away from me and now at the end it had finally come back.

I recalled the oath that I had taken when they had pinned the badge to my heart.

'Guard thy badge with your life and honour, for this badge is now part of you as much as the most vital parts of your being.'

At Residency School, badges were the most precious treasures, a cumulative reward for years of hard work, sweat, tears, victories and defeats. Vikram, in a testament of his love, had given her the badge, and now she had passed it on to me. I held my badge, now dark with rust, and I couldn't fathom why this badge, this bauble, could mean so much, then, now and forever more.

In the end, when I left school, I had made a vow never to cry again. Nobody else but Riya would ever deserve my tears. I had stuck to my vow, and I had not let myself cry, not when my grandparents died, not when I didn't get the job I wanted, not when I had failed time and time again. But I am crying now, laughing and crying, fingering the badge, feeling joy, gratitude, happiness, release. These were the tears I had almost cried when I got married, the tears I had almost cried when my son was born, the tears I almost cried when I made my first million. I had never let myself cry, but now I cried because confronting death made me now want to live.

If Riya had never died, my life would have been a simple mountain stream, coursing a simple path, but she had pushed that stream to merge into a vast ocean, and I knew that my life was about something bigger than what I had once thought it would be.

I realize there is a greater force than us, something that shapes our lives, guiding us, helping us. I realize that life wasn't meant to be fought, but cherished, for who knew when the last moment would arrive. As Riya had once told me, life was for living, and death, that was for dying, and even that was beautiful in its own way. I didn't have to be afraid of death, but I had to be prepared to face it, and I could only do that by living the best life that I could.

Riya had thirty days to live and when she went, she went with acceptance, knowing that her short life had been lived fully and well. That was the thing with her – she taught you things when you didn't even want to learn, she made you laugh when you really wanted to cry, she made you live when all you wanted to do was to die.

Acknowledgements

There are many whom I have to thank for making this book what it has become. My gurus, my yoga practice, my family. But most of all I want to thank Nicholas Henderson for being there for me from start to end. This book wouldn't have been half of what it is without you. Thank you for being there at conception, encouraging me to write it, hearing me out when the going was hard, for stepping in as the editor and, most of all, for always being there at the end of the line.

Acknowledgements

[illegible]